Mick Farren is a musician, an underground journalist and a novelist. He ran the underground paper IT for two years and, with designer Edward Barker, produced a book on the politics of rock called WATCH OUT KIDS. At the same time, again with Barker, he brought out the first British underground comic, NASTY TALES. The comic was the subject of an obscenity case at the Old Bailey which ended – after a time lag of nearly two years – in acquittal. Mick Farren is also the author of THE TALE OF WILLY'S RATS.

Also by Mick Farren
in Mayflower Books

THE TALE OF WILLY'S RATS

The Texts of Festival

Mick Farren

Mayflower

Granada Publishing Limited
First published in 1975 by Mayflower Books Ltd
Frogmore, St Albans, Herts AL2 2NF

First published in Great Britain by
Hart-Davis, MacGibbon Ltd 1973
Copyright © Mick Farren 1973
Made and printed in Great Britain by
Richard Clay (The Chaucer Press) Ltd
Bungay, Suffolk
Set in Linotype Georgian

I

The marshland had run for a day's walk. A day had passed since he had come down from the hill country. Three days of slipping through his home hill land, skirting the inhabited valleys, avoiding the grim herders who clawed a living from the corroded hills and grew savage in their isolation. And then a cold, dirty day trudging through the lowland swamp, picking a way on the broken paved surface where swamp rats squalled and slid away as he approached.

Every now and then he would stumble as he missed the paved surface and his foot would sink into soft slime. Oily water would pour over the top of his father's high boots. Cursing, he would drag his leg out of the slime and poke around with his toe to find where the paving started again. Sometimes it would prove to be a broad crack in the surface and then it would be necessary to wade waist-deep in the slime until he had regained the ancient stone pavement which, although befouled, was at least solid. Crossing them was also complicated by the unknown depth of these cracks and by the need to draw his knife and the family piece from his belt and hold them safe from the poisonous waters.

The sun set and a close blanket of mist, high as a man's hip, lay on the surface of the swamp. Mosquitoes danced on the damp air, flitting their elaborate rituals in and out of the shadows cast by the mesa-like ruins.

The darkness was starting to close in and still he had gained no sight of the legendary raised highway that ran straight to Festival.

The rats grew bold and brambles caught at his legs. He gave thanks to the women of his village who had presented him with his leather trousers at the spring laying on. The token that had paid tribute to his separate, restless ego was now mud-spattered. A long way from their previous splendour, his trousers were at last proving useful.

A rising moon, bloated and orange, gave him a minimal light by which to find his footsteps, but at the same time distracted him with a multitude of black shadows and glinting highlights that hinted at an undefined menace.

A rat darted behind the rotting teeth of a corroded iron wagon frame. The man started, drew his gun and then froze with shame as the rat vanished, cleaving a short-lived V in black water. He had been entrusted with the piece of his house. The token of his father's power in the tribe had been given to arm him on his absurd quest. Now he was waving it around like a spooked fool, about to waste one of the twenty man-killing shells on a rat. He was yielding to the dark and to paranoia. He put his hand on the pouch around his neck but then withdrew it. Although he was frightened, although he was lost in the black night of the swamps of 'Ndunn, it was not a crisis that would merit the use of either ammunition or the crystals. He must face his fear alone. He must weather a hard night in this western swamp; it was the path to Festival and its ancient skills. He shivered at the damp; holstered his gun; pulled his cloak closer round his shoulders but the coarse wool, with its mends and patches, held the water and afforded him little warmth as he felt for the next step on the pavement.

All night he trudged on. Repeatedly losing his footing; skirting the worst fissures until he could sidetrack no longer and was forced to ford the intervening water. As dawn began to cut through the mist on the swamp he paused to rest, sitting hunched on a moss-covered square of masonry.

The clearing of the mist gradually revealed a dark line almost at the horizon. It ran across the marsh, almost parallel to the direction the man imagined he had taken in the darkness. Its apparent straightness seemed to indicate that it was fashioned by men, some artifact of the oldtime city. It was by no means the broad pillared highway of legend. It was, as far as he could see, merely a straight, raised embankment. Even if it was not the true road, it

8

would make easier going than the marsh wading of the previous day.

With renewed hope he made his way painfully to the distant ridge. By the time he reached the roadway – and a roadway it proved to be as he came nearer – the sun was high and the swamp water reflected it like a pitted, dirty mirror. The drying mud irritated his skin and ran in dirty rivulets as he sweated.

Sick and exhausted he clawed through the brambles that clung thickly to the side of the banking.

The top of the bank proved to be a broad paved road, straight and smooth, although heavily overgrown with moss and nettles. Its length was here and there dotted with the rusting hulks of oldtime iron wagons.

Having at last raised himself above the level of the poisonous swamp, the man finally felt safe to rest. He stripped off his cloak and jacket and bundled them into a pillow, then removed his belt with its gun and knife, laid it close to his right hand and settled down to sleep.

*   *   *

It was afternoon before Jo-Jo rested. The pursuit must have been called off long before dawn and it was not fear that had kept him walking; it was the shame of the loser tag that forced him to place distance between himself and Festival.

It had looked like an open and shut mugging when he had approached the fat crystal dealer on the outside of Shacktown, but as he had pulled his knife six retainers had appeared out of nowhere and started him running. He had kept going all night, fearing that they might have rented mounts. A lot of merchants were really heavy on the idea of bringing in muggers. Thieves these days were treated a whole lot different from the heroes of the texts.

It wasn't as though he was even a full-time thief. He'd only laid for the fat dealer in order to get a stake. Everyone who went freewheeling got down on their luck. There were countless texts on that very situation. What really made him keep on walking, stuck on a nowhere road in the 'Ndunn marshes, was the inescapable fact that by blowing the mugging he had once again strengthened the image of Jo-Jo the loser.

Finally physical tiredness overcame his self-reproach and he sank down on a rusty, moss-covered wheel, a discarded leftover from the oldtime autos. He pulled out his pipe and reached inside his cotton shirt, itself a relic of the great times, for his battered weed pouch. He had no food but he could at least smoke, although even that would only last for two or three pipes.

When the pipe was finished, he tapped out the ash on the stones at his feet. He felt a good deal more relaxed although, he had to admit, he was in a pretty sound mess. He decided he might as well keep moving while the sun was high. It would be unwise to return to Festival, especially if he were broke, so his best bet was to press on and see where the marsh road led. Maybe he would find some village where he could put himself back together. In any case the marsh was beginning to trip his fears most bitterly and he would sooner be through it. Out of reach of its stench and the black ruins that squatted in the poisoned waters.

He stood up, stretched and started walking slowly down the raised highway. The sun was hot on the back of his neck, his stomach reminded him that he was hungry and he began to curse his luck again. The words of a text, half-remembered from childhood, came strongly to his mind.

'If it wasn't for bad luck
I wouldn't have no luck at all.'

As a child in the village he had been quick and popular. He and the other children had sat round the ancient circuits and listened to the texts over and over until they could recite them.

'Listen and learn,' his father had said, 'for the circuits will die and we will have to remember.'

Jo-Jo had been quick to learn, quicker than the other

10

village kids. His father had been pleased. He had smoked his pipe and boasted how his son would some day be a mighty man.

Maybe it had been that same quickness that had caused him to break out of the village when the great hunger had come. He had studied the texts.

'Run, run, run' they urged him.

And he had run, leaving his neighbours to die by inches, fighting to cultivate their barren hillside.

By degrees he had run to Festival. Caught and intoxicated by its swarming humanity he had run with the crowd, hustling, gambling, stealing, until he was chased back to the road again, still running.

But running was a state of mind by mid-afternoon; the best he could manage physically was a steady trudge. Stones had ripped his canvas boots and it was beginning to seem as though he had walked forever when he first saw the man.

The man lay in the road. He wore the coarse homespun shirt and leather trousers that were the standard dress of the young stud from the hills, and the greasy plaits and coloured headband marked him as fresh out of one of the villages that huddled in the valleys of the bare downs to the south.

At first Jo-Jo thought he was dead but, as he cautiously approached, the clothes bunched into a pillow and the gun belt within reach of an outstretched hand all left him in no doubt that the man was merely sleeping. When he saw the gun, his mind reeled. A piece. With a piece of his own he could go back to Festival walking like a man.

Jo-Jo dropped into a crouch and drew his knife. Silently he stalked the sleeping man. A rube fresh out of the hills, probably carrying the family gun with hillbilly pride. This country boy could be exactly what he needed for his new start. Maybe his losing streak was over.

Suddenly, when Jo-Jo was not three paces from the man, a bird, alarmed at his approach, flapped croaking out of the brambles.

The man woke and reached for his gun at the sight of the gaunt figure with its long knife. Jo-Jo froze in horror as the big barrel swung up.

The hammer came back as he squeezed the trigger. Squeeze, don't snatch at it, his father had told him.

The hammer snapped home with a click. The gun hadn't fired.

Jo-Jo laughed. A rube with his treasured family pistol and hundred-year-old ammunition. His shells had probably been useless for thirty years.

Jo-Jo laughed again and slashed at the man's throat.

Too shocked even to be afraid, the man fell back and died.

II

Old Johanna, wife of Aaron the gunmaker, sat and rocked in the doorway of her tent. A stylised pistol once painted on the ancient canvas had been almost bleached to nothing by the sun and obscured by generations of mismatched patching. She didn't worry that the canvas would soon decay altogether. By then Aaron would have been able to extend the wooden-built forge to include their living quarters.

She was content and life treated her kindly in her old age. The slightly acrid smell of molten metal reached her as her eldest, Vernon, moulded bullets on the small furnace in the back of the tent, and flies buzzed lazily in the sunlight around the garbage heap to the side of the tent.

The great swirling texts had little meaning for her life now. It was almost like when she was a child. The small texts held their prime meaning for the very young and very old. The favourite had become the one she now hummed, drawing deeply on her pipe:

> 'Throw my troubles out the door
> I don't need them anymore.'

It was like being a child again, only this time she did not have the years of fear to follow. It had taken years for her to dare even to recall the terror and even now she avoided it.

It was pleasant to recall her girlhood: seeking wild weed and herbs that her mother sold to travellers; listening to her mother telling the cards and reading stars for dealers and stagelords who came to their cottage with their fine clothes and tall horses; and the winter nights when laughing strangers would produce silver flasks of spirit from their fur cloaks and sport with her mother while she lay in a cot tucked up in skins and blankets. It was pleasant, too, to remember how, as a mature woman, she had taken Aaron as a husband and the pride with which she had taken charge of his trading. Didn't all the neighbours say that although Aaron was a master gunmaker, it was old Johanna who took care of business?

It was the years in between that she tried never to let pass through her mind. After years of security, the pain was still too strong for her to be able to cope with the memory of the day when the Christies had broken into her mother's tiny home.

She herself, at the time a young girl, had heard the rumours of how Peter the Blessed had raised his legion of Christ and roamed the country, destroying outlying home-steads and burning those who told the cards and made ceremony at the trees.

Of course, they had never thought it could happen to them. They had believed the Christie fanaticism would pass like the other fads. They had gone on believing it until the day that the Christies came.

She had been sitting in front of the cottage when they had stormed up the lane. The memory was so clear and vivid: the sunlight, the dusty earth in front of the cottage where the goat was tethered and the chickens scratched. Then suddenly they had flooded the lane, dozens of them in their dirty white robes, screaming their cursed text.

Howling 'All you need is love', they had kicked her aside and dragged her mother out of the cottage.

Johanna shuddered. It was too late now to stop the mem-ory; she should never have started such thoughts. It flooded back, how they had held her and smashed down the cottage to make fuel for their awful bonfire. How they had kindled the heaped, broken timbers and bundles of thatch, bound her and her mother, dragged her mother to the flames while she was forced to watch and then flogged her until her mother's screams had completely ceased. Above all she remembered the staring eyes and sweating faces that had stood round her in the dust after it was over and the hoarse voice that told her that Christ loved her. She remembered their leaving and the night of weeping in the ashes.

Then had come the painful journey into Festival to beg and steal and later to become a listless whore on the Drag. A time when the only punctuation had been a fierce joy at the news that Joe Starkweather had led his men out of the western commune and massacred the Christies in the October battle.

She finally met Aaron though and loved him. They had brought up their children in the gunmaker's trade; the giving had been good and the dark years had been put behind.

There were the times, however, when remembering could not be totally avoided.

Old Johanna's painful reverie was stopped as she noticed the lengthening shadows and she rose to busy herself inside the tent. Aaron would soon return hungry from the metal dealers.

As she replaced her pipe in the pouch on her belt, a small furtive man hurried out of the shadows. He wore a dirty, mud-caked cloak many sizes too large and the bushy red hair that framed his rodent face was matted with dust. She backed towards the tent door, ready to call for Vernon.

Jo-Jo stared at the old woman. She looked spooked by him; maybe he looked more beat up than he imagined. He came quickly to the point.

''Ave any filled thirty-eights?'

Although when on his own, or talking with young women, he used the purer hill dialect of his own village, he now adopted the rough tongue of common Festival to bargain with this stout matron. The woman stopped edging towards the tent door and eyed him sharply.

'Filled thirty-eights? You got trades?'

'I got empties fo' trades.'

The woman eyed him suspiciously. Ammunition was the high currency of Festival. By his appearance Johanna hardly expected him to have either bar room or dealer script, let alone real shells.

'How many empties?'

'Twenty.'

Johanna thought quickly. The man appeared to have no place holding even dead shells: his canvas leggings indicated that he didn't have the price of a pair of boots. He was probably a mugger or heistman. She saw the chance of a quick profit.

'Six filled fo' twenty empty.'

'You rip me off, ol' woman, I could get twelve for twenty in tomorra's market.'

'Get to market then.'

Johanna made as if to go into the tent. Jo-Jo spoke quickly.

'Wait, I need filled shells tonight. Maybe I take ten.'

Johanna stopped and looked him up and down.

'Eight.'

Jo-Jo hesitated; perhaps he could get nine. Johanna began to look impatient. Jo-Jo changed his mind; eight was better than nothing.

'Done.'

Johanna leaned into the tent and shouted:

'Vernon! Bring out eight filled thirty-eights.' She turned to Jo-Jo. 'You got the empties?'

Jo-Jo handed over the twenty dead shells. Almost immediately a boy – he judged him to be about fifteen – emerged from the tent and gave his mother a handful of bullets. Johanna counted them into Jo-Jo's hand.

'You sure these're good?'

Jo-Jo shot the old woman a suspicious glance as he thumbed the shells into his belt. The woman glared at him.

'My husband's a master gunsmith, we don't rip off honest folk.'

'Okay, okay, I just asked.'

Jo-Jo hurried off. Johanna ducked inside the tent and rubbed her hands on her homespun smock. The evening meal would be late but she couldn't have turned down that end-of-the-day profit.

* * *

Jo-Jo hurried towards the Drag. It was almost dark, and braziers and rubbish fires blazed every four or five paces. The avenues between the squat tents and single-storey wooden shacks were illuminated by their dull glow and the acrid smoke that drifted and billowed across his path.

He was some way from the Drag and he decided to take a chance on cutting through the Merchants' Quarter.

In front of a lavish tent of matched hides, supported by stout carved and polished poles, a chained dog barked and snarled at him. Two armed retainers emerged from the tent and Jo-Jo slid into the shadows and crouched very still. Word of his flight might have spread and he could not afford to get careless. After peering into the smoky gloom for a while, one of the retainers cursed the dog and then went back inside. Jo-Jo scuttled away.

The torches that lined the Drag were almost welcoming. He began to walk straighter, conscious of the gun on his hip and secure in the familiar dim lights that shone out of the doorways and across the porches of the big, wooden pleasure houses that lined the dirty, crowded streets. The sound of music and raucous laughter reassured him as he avoided the drunks and beggars who thronged the steps to the gambling joints and whore houses. There in Festival's red-light district he was safe, unless the lord's men should mount a full-scale raid and that seldom if ever happened.

Fingers from the darkness tugged at Jo-Jo's cloak.

'Wanna space fo' fun, stranger?'

Jo-Jo spun round. A youngish woman with the hard smile of the full-time whore stood looking at him. She let her brown, shapeless wrap drop open to display a flash of white breasts and stomach. Jo-Jo grinned.

'Later, babe, later.'

He'd have a dozen whores at the end of the night but right now his luck was running and he was going to clean up.

'Okay honey, don't say you missed out.'

The girl swayed off looking for johns more anxious to play. Jo-Jo moved on, no longer hurrying but content to stroll and savour the atmosphere of the Drag. In front of Harry Krishna's Last Chance he paused. Maybe he should start with a couple of the smaller joints and build up a stake, but then again he had eight shells and the piece for capital. Why not start at the top?

Jo-Jo marched up to the swing doors.

The heat, noise, and smell of weed and spirit hit Jo-Jo like a physical force. Flickering lamps swung under the low-beamed roof and were reflected by the big cracked mirror behind the bar. A guitar player sat on a small raised platform and tried desperately to be heard above the conversation of the fifty or so drifters, hustlers, whores and tribesmen who thronged the bar and crowded around the half-dozen gambling tables.

The people in any gambling joint can be divided into two strict groups, the hunters and the prey, and although individuals may swap roles the rule remains absolute. One man who prided himself on always running with the hunt was Frankie Lee.

Frankie Lee sat at his table with the air of a man who owned it. It was the table where everyone knew they could find him; where he took care of business and he ran the game.

He wore a black velvet frock coat, the kind of pre-disaster relic that marked the successful gambler. The tight raw-hide trousers and high-heeled boots also had marks of a hustler who had made it, as did the gold earring that glinted as he brushed back his mass of black curly hair. The look of money made him seem taller than his true height which was only medium, and his sharp, weather-beaten face had the look of one who spends a lot of time knowing or at least bluffing that he is right.

Through the weed smoke and between the line of men and women at the bar, Frankie had noticed the furtive form of Jo-Jo come in. Maybe the loser had ripped himself a stake. Frankie had taken Jo-Jo three times before, this hill boy who fancied himself as a hotshot card player. No matter how he tried to hide his country ways, that Jo-Jo was a rube loser. Frankie sat and waited; Jo-Jo would be over to play him.

Before coming into the Chance Jo-Jo had jacked four of his shells into the gun. That left him four to play with. He put them on the counter in front of the barkeep.

'Change these into script.'

'Sure,' the barkeep shuffled away and returned to dump a small pile of tokens and paper on the bar. Jo-Jo pushed a single token towards him.

'Brew.'

The barkeep handed Jo-Jo a mug of beer. Jo-Jo turned, beer in hand, and faced the room. On the far side of the room Frankie Lee pretended not to notice him. Tonight, Jo-Jo thought, tonight I'll clean out that superior mother. He swallowed his beer and made his way through the crowd to where Frankie sat.

'Hi there, Frankie Lee.'

'Greetin' rube, have a seat.'

Frankie Lee grinned at him, flashing his gold tooth. Yeah, thought Jo-Jo, tonight you are really going to pay for riding me. Frankie riffled the deck of worn dirty cards.

'What's your pleasure, rube?'

Jo-Jo hesitated and to cover his indecision he leaned back in his chair. Frankie grinned again as though he knew his ploy.

'How about twocard kid? That your strength?'

'Suits me.'

'You sure? It could cost you.'

Jo-Jo reached inside his cloak and pulled out the handful of papers and tokens, dropping them on the table.

'Strong enough to start?'

Frankie was stuffing his pipe with weed. He struck a flame, inhaled and blew smoke across the table towards Jo-Jo. In the centre of its wooden top, stained black by a century of spilled alcohol, was a deck of dirty, dog-eared cards.

'Yeah – cut to deal?'

Frankie tapped them.

'Why not.'

Jo-Jo turned up a seven; Frankie showed a jack and reached for the cards. He called a low ante and Jo-Jo slid a handful of tokens across the table. Frankie Lee dealt the cards.

*   *   *

Frankie had won the first game but the pot had remained small. Jo-Jo then won the next three in a row. The first two had been worth very little, but the third had built a little and Jo-Jo began to suspect that his feeling on the road had been correct. Frankie won the next and for the three hands after Jo-Jo did nothing, folding immediately. Then Jo-Jo was dealt a pair and forced up the bidding against Frankie's queen. Frankie had no second queen and the pot gave Jo-Jo double the script that he had brought to the table.

As the size of stakes started to increase, a small knot of drifters and bar girls formed around the table, the majority standing behind Frankie Lee, watching his cards. There was little action on the next few games and the spectators began to drift back to the bar or the faster play of the dice table.

Before the next game Frankie yelled for a drink and Jo-Jo began to feel a sense of elation. After the hole cards had been dealt he paused before making his bet.

'Frankie, you don't look too happy, old buddy.'

Frankie stared coldly at Jo-Jo.

'Make your bet, rube.'

'Hold on there old buddy. Give me a filla weed.' Jo-Jo paused as he picked up Frankie's pouch. 'Ain't that my country ways are gettin' to you? Ain't that, is it old buddy?'

Jo-Jo put a flame to his pipe and inhaled. For a second he held his breath, then he blew very deliberately at Frankie who scowled and said nothing. Jo-Jo looked at his hole card. It was a ten. Slowly and with care Jo-Jo divided his money into four equal piles; then he pushed one of the piles into the centre of the table. Frankie met the bet. The pile of money in front of him was dwindling rapidly. With a rigid face he dealt the second cards. Jo-Jo showed a queen and Frankie a seven. Jo-Jo grinned, expecting Frankie to fold. Instead he checked and Jo-Jo, still grinning, slid the second of his four piles across the table. But still Frankie Lee didn't fold. Using all the money he had left on the table, he raised Jo-Jo's bet. Jo-Jo's rat-grin faded a little but, still smiling, he put his two remaining piles into the middle. Frankie had no more money; he had to fold this time. But Frankie was reaching inside his shirt, pulling out a wad of papers. He was raising the bet again.

Doubt rushed into Jo-Jo's mind. Maybe he was holding a pair. He pushed back the idea. It was his night and he had everything on these cards. It was too late to fold. It was his night; he had to win.

Jo-Jo stood up. He undid his gunbelt and laid it on the pile of money.

'I'm callin' you, Frankie, I reckon that covers the bet.'

Frankie said nothing. He just smiled and turned over an ace.

Jo-Jo went limp. No, it couldn't be, it couldn't be. He'd blown it. His hand darted for the gun.

Before Jo-Jo had even pulled the gun clear of the belt, a little single-shot ball gun had appeared in Frankie Lee's hand. The round ball had taken Jo-Jo in the chest, knocking him back into his chair. For a moment he had hung there and then the chair toppled and he hit the floor.

In that moment Jo-Jo realised that, if his run of luck had really ever started, it was now finished for good.

III

The spread fingers were rigid on the wooden table. The knife was a blur as it rose and fell, stabbing viciously at the spaces between the fingers. The men in the tent finished the chant with a shout and Nath stood back from the table, wiping the sweat from his shaved head. Dimly he was pleased that his turn in the knife game was safely over, for, although proud of his speed, old Wob had lost a finger not long ago. He was content to chant with the rest.

Oltha sat in a carved chair in front of the table where the men played the knife game. Apart from straw, rugs and two large chests, the table and chair were the only furniture in the tent, in fact the only furniture in the whole camp, the property of the chief – tokens of his authority, carefully carried from place to place in the rear wagon.

About fifteen men crowded the tent, some standing, some sprawled in the straw. They were short, thickset men with coarse, brutal faces, and either shaved heads or long straggling hair, greased down with animal fat and gathered into heavy plaits wound with strips or rags. They had a standard dress of a coarse woollen or hide tunic: a sleeveless one-piece garment ornamented with crude brooches or studs and their leggings were bound up with thick strips of leather. Their bare arms were covered with tattoos, birds, animals, skulls, and women in obscene poses; and their faces carried the marks of a hard, bestial, outdoor life.

A few were already snoring; the hill farmer's beer was taking its toll and would ensure that the game did not last all night, although it was likely that fights would break out before the last man collapsed. Fights, however, broke out most nights in camp and it was as well that the men were unconscious while the moon was still high. At dawn they would have to break camp and make the long day's journey to the meeting place.

Outside the tent the remainder of the mounted guns stood watch, lounged by the fire or grappled with a woman in the deep shadows. The deal of beer had turned the camp into a party and around the twenty fires or in the dozen squat, conical tents figures shouted, sang and stumbled. Even the guards grew lax.

It was as well that they were partying tonight. The next few days would be given to travelling and fighting.

He stood up and the knife chant faltered. The man with his hand spread in the candlelight stopped his stabbing and straightened.

''Nuff?'

''Nuff,' confirmed Oltha, 'soonly I sleep. March tomorrow.'

The men nodded and filed out of the tent. For a while he sat in the empty tent. He listened to the shouts as the men from the tent joined their brothers round the fire. Oltha scratched his stomach and felt pleased. His tribe was becoming strong. Not, of course, as strong as in his grandfather's day. He dimly remembered the legendary time: how once the guns had ridden the roaring iron monsters that sped across the land. In his grandfather's day the tribe had been invincible; even the lords of Festival had feared their might and paid tribute. But the iron monsters had one by one died until, even when he was a child, only five had remained. As he grew their magic had failed and the stocks of the spirit had dwindled. Then had come the defeat in the west; the last two machines had been destroyed. The warriors, his father among them, had fallen before Starkweather's army and their repeating guns and he became chief of a broken tribe, outcasts on the barren, spoiled hills.

Gradually they had regained their strength, raiding farms, absorbing small warrior bands and attacking hill settlements.

Of course many had died in their wanderings, particularly the children, but gradually the power of the tribe grew. They raided towns, taking weapons, supplies and women captives to swell the tribe. The tribe stood at thirty mounted guns, seventy archers and two hundred foot warriors. With the power of the alliance they would take tribute from Festival for the first time in two generations. Oltha stood up and pushed through the tent flap. The warriors round the fire greeted him; one passed him a jug of beer. He drained it and spat in the fire. Maybe they wouldn't stop at tribute; maybe they would take Festival itself.

Oltha stalked through the camp. Silhouetted against the fire light, dark figures swayed and stumbled between the rough hide tents, and smoke drifted close to the ground. Occasionally it would billow up and catch his throat. A huge warrior pumped at a woman on the ground in Oltha's path. Urgently they forced themselves at each other; the woman, head thrown back and a white leg clasped across the warrior's back, looked with unseeing eyes at Oltha as he grinned and stepped round.

Indeed, with the added strength of Iggy and his hard crystal boys, maybe they would take Festival. Of course the alliance would not last. The crystal madness of Iggy's gang would quickly lead to fighting. With luck most of them would die in the battle. Their wild-eyed killing was awesome but their madness also led to massive losses. Oltha could deal with Iggy. Oltha could deal with the world.

Pressed against a tree one of old Peg's brood, a leggy teenager with small hard breasts, struggled with a short fat bowman.

Oltha approached them, spun the man round by his shoulder and hit him once across the mouth with his fist in its studded leather glove. The man crashed into the base of the tree and slid to a sitting position, wiping blood from his lips. Oltha laughed and, seizing the girl round the waist, slapped her backside and half dragged, half carried her back to his tent.

*   *   *

By the time the sun stood clear of the hills the tribe was on the move. In single file they had come down from the hillside and formed up to march in open formation along the broad valley.

The mounted guns came first, abreast of each other in a broad line. Behind them a wide loose column of the foot men. On either flank a line of archers watched the hill slopes and then the wagons and a straggle of women, children and animals.

Oltha sat on his pony in the centre of the line of horsemen.

For most of the morning they moved slowly down the valley. The sun grew hot. Oltha sweated in his leather shirt. The studs chafed his shoulder blades. Beneath him the pony plodded across the hard ground and sparse grass. Beside them a river wound sluggishly down the valley, its banks lined with weed beds where mosquitoes danced.

At the end of the valley Oltha ordered a stop and women served a meal of dried meat, cheese and hard bread, and another deal of beer was distributed. They ate hurriedly and then reformed into a long column to cross the hills. By mid-afternoon they halted at the top of the line of hills. On the other side of the valley beneath them was the settlement where Iggy and his men had turned a tribe of hill farmers into their slaves.

Oltha sent his scouts ahead.

*   *   *

The crash of boots on the front porch roused Iggy from his nod. Winston was yelling in his ear, going too fast for him to make intelligence of it.

'Cool off, mutha, whassa matta?'

'Looks like they're a-comin'.'

'You sho'?'

'Sho'.'

'Whereabouts?'

'Top of that hill, bro' Iggy.'

25

'No shit?'

'An' scouts a-comin'.'

Iggy giggled and stood up.

'Round up the boys, an' get the signal t'gether. Ri'?'

'Ri' on.'

Winston thundered off and Iggy yelled for a villager to get him a jug of water and sluiced it over his face and neck. The hill boy stood looking at him, scared and awkward.

'Whatcha starin' at, mutha, ain'tcha got no work?'

Iggy aimed a kick at the hill boy who scuttled away; then he buckled on his gun, pulled his wide brimmed hat over his eyes and stepped down into the village square. He was aware that he cut an impressive figure in front of his men. He had class. His black silk shirt was an antique, as were his high boots while the black trousers of finished leather with the silver studs down the outside seams had belonged to one of the sharpest dressers in Festival until he had taken a fancy to them. His hard eyes, which contrasted so strikingly with the soft femininity of the rest of his face, scanned the dusty square of the little village. He scowled; it was little more than a collection of brick and thatch cottages grouped around a well and a square of beaten earth. He knew that he could do better than this. At his signal a villager brought his horse.

Men started to assemble in the village square as Winston spread the word. Iggy selected seven of his top guns and told them to saddle up. A pillar of smoke rose from the signal fire. Oltha would be coming in. Iggy grinned and sniffed a small pinch of crystal. Winston hurried across the square.

'Break out the repeaters.'

'Sho' Iggy.'

'An' load 'em.'

'Sho'.'

The seven men whom Iggy had selected returned with their horses; then Winston led a party of villagers who carried the eight priceless rapid-fire guns into the square.

26

'Okay, each of yous take a repeater; we gonna blow Oltha when he sees us.'

The guns were handed out and Iggy turned to Winston.

'Get the rest of the boys spread out, an' wait. Okay?'

'Okay.'

Iggy mounted and the troop of eight rode out of the village.

*　　　*　　　*

Oltha's tribe wound its way down the hillside. The scouts had spotted the signal and Oltha had moved the tribe. At the front, his ten best guns bunched behind him, Oltha looked back at the whole tribe. If it was a trap there was no way back. They would have to fight their way out of it.

As they neared the foot of the slope Oltha saw Iggy and his men sitting motionless by a small clump of trees perhaps three hundred paces distant. Oltha raised his hand and one by one the tribe halted. For a while they paused, peering across the valley at their future allies; then Oltha kicked his pony and, motioning to the ten to follow, thundered across the grass to where Iggy and his seven riders sat waiting.

Iggy watched, his face blank as the tribesmen galloped towards them. Only the occasional twitch of the black gloved hands showed the tension and the hits of crystal he had been through on the way to this meeting.

With ten paces between the two groups, Oltha halted his men. They wheeled their ponies flashily, making them rear and throw up divots of turf. Then they formed into a line and Oltha walked his pony slowly forward. Iggy, equally slowly, rode out from the shadow of the copse to meet him. Facing each other they halted.

'Greetings from the tribe of Oltha.'

'Hi there, ride t'village?'

Oltha dispatched a man to bring in the tribe. Then he and Iggy rode off towards the village. The two groups of horsemen fell in together and followed them.

27

Nath covertly eyed the men who rode amongst his brothers. They looked ill-fed, thin, gaunt, with staring eyes; although their rich clothes, larger mounts and the fact that, to a man, they carried rapid-fire guns belied any suggestion of poverty.

Iggy and Oltha rode side by side. Iggy surreptitiously glanced at the hill chief. These hill boys were a mean bunch, with their short shaggy ponies and rough leather clothes. With these hick butchers he could run rings through Festival. There would be a problem in controlling them, of course. At least until he had them strung out on crystal and that wouldn't be easy. By the look of the mob coming down the hill there must be a few hundred of them and the chief would probably know enough to suspect if he went around handing the stuff out like candy. The first stage would be to turn on his roughest boys. After that, if the chief gave any trouble, he could safely waste him.

Iggy yelled a question at the silent chief.

'How many have ya brought?'

The chief looked at him as though figuring in his head.

'Three times hundred.'

Iggy grinned to himself. He had guessed right.

'Countin' women?'

'More, with women.'

'Ri' on. You betta pick a buncha land on the edge of the village. Betta camp there. Git y'self togetha an' come 'n' party. Ri'?'

Oltha grunted and gathered his men to select a camp for the tribe. Iggy and his escort rode back to the village, casting long shadows.

*   *   *

Outside what had been the house of the village headman, Iggy and Oltha watched their men party in the village square. The atmosphere was subdued, each side viewing the presence of so many strangers as a potential threat. Oltha had only permitted his horsemen to come into the village.

The remaining bulk of his men he had ordered to stay with the tents. Oltha no longer expected an immediate trap but it paid to be careful. If most of Iggy's men were in the square it meant that he had about seventy under his control and the size of the horsepens signified that all were mounted. Finally Iggy broke the silence.

'You wanna go inside an' talk?'

Oltha nodded.

Inside the house two village women served them with beer, corn spirit and oat cakes, and once they were alone Iggy brought a chair to one side of the fire that blazed in the wide stone hearth and indicated that Oltha should seat himself. The fire threw flickering patterns on the beamed ceiling. Iggy picked up a small carved box from the mantel shelf. Opening it he sniffed a small hit of crystal, hesitated and offered the open box to the hill chief. Oltha shook his head and Iggy grinned, shut the box and returned it to the shelf.

'You reckon to take Festival.'

Iggy shrugged.

'Why not?'

'T' hold or t' loot?'

'Either, work it out when we get there.'

'When do we start?'

'Hold it, hold it. Not so fast.'

'Why wait? We ride to Festival. We fight. No reason to wait.'

'You ain't that dumb. We gotta lot needs doing. That's why wait.'

Oltha said nothing. There was the sound of shouts and laughter. Iggy stood up and walked to the window. The groups of men who had previously stayed with their own kind were gradually beginning to mingle. When the hill boys got drunk there would probably be fights. Winston's squad would take care of that if it became necessary. Iggy turned to face the fire.

'The first thing we're gonna need is supplies an' an easy fight so we can see how our boys work out togetha, ri'?'

Oltha nodded.

'An' I got a deal that'd take care of both those.'

Oltha looked puzzled.

'No easy raids left in this country. Too near Festival.'

'There's a caravan, four days out from the great bridge, four days out on the old road headed for Festival.'

Oltha slowly leaned forward, a wolfish grin spreading over his face.

'A caravan?'

'Ri', a caravan. An' in two days it'll cross Ruined Hill, not a morning's ride from here. First we take the caravan. After that we head for Festival. Agree?'

'Agree.'

Iggy again took the carved box from the mantel. He took another hit of crystal, hesitated, glanced at Oltha and replaced the box.

IV

'Hey wagonmaster, you wanna join us for a game of stud?' one of the skinners called to him out of the gathering dark.

'Leave me out Charlie; I ain't got the head for it tonight.'

'Okay.' Charlie disappeared round the side of a wagon.

The wagons were formed into their protective circle and for Big Eddie the day was over. But he still felt tense and uneasy. Five days out from the Great Bridge. No trouble, except the big puller throwing a piston coupling. With only three days to Festival it was unlikely there would be trouble but still the feeling remained; nothing that he could put his finger on, just a bad feeling.

And there had been rumours. Again nothing very tangible. Just an increasing number of reports of bandit tribes moving south. The crystal-freak gangs getting bigger. It was almost as though the wolves were hungry in the hills and moving on the town. Only the town was Festival and the predators were human. If that was the case it was going to make a wagonmaster's job a great deal more difficult, particularly as most dealers were too concerned with profit margins to provide a solid escort for their caravans.

Eddie shrugged. If anything was going to happen it would probably be when they crossed Broken Hill the next morning. After that they'd be in Festival territory proper and there'd be nothing to worry about.

Eddie climbed the iron ladder to the small sleeping cabin at the rear of the big puller's great black iron boiler. Inside the little cabin Danny Junior, the stoker, sprawled in his bunk in his vest and leggings, his heavy fur-lined jacket hanging from a nail and the rich smell of good Brissol weed filling the cabin.

'Hey chief, wanna pipe? You look on a down.'

'No' now kid, where's Mac?'

'I dunno, mebbe in a card game. He shut down steam an' wandered off.'

'I wanna make an early start. You better get the fire going before dawn.'

'I was gonna crash soon, so tha's okay. What's the trouble, though, chief? We've come five days from the Bridge, it's been real easy.'

'No trouble, I just got a bad feelin', I wanna make an early start.'

'I never heard you bitch before about a trip bein' too easy.'

'Yeah well, maybe I'm gettin' old.'

'Mebbe you been pushin' caravans too long, mebbe you should settle down in Festival. Join the stageguards.'

'An' get fat? Sure.'

Eddie pulled off his steel-shod boots and climbed into his bunk.

'It's a good life bein' a solja, so they say.'

'Those fools swaggerin' round Festival in their fancy surcoats. They ain't soljas. I should know, I was in a real army.'

'When was you in an army?'

Eddie paused.

'I rode with Joe Starkweather, years ago, when I was just a kid.'

'No kiddin', when he put down the Christies?'

'Yeah, an' when he breaked the tribes.'

'Shit.'

Danny puffed on his pipe. Starkweather and the commune army were almost a legend and now he finds out that old Eddie was with them. The world was pretty strange.

'How come you never settled in Festival when Joe led his people outta the commune?'

Eddie thought for a while. When they had followed Joe to Festival, after the commune had lapsed into isolationism and dogma, he had the chance. Most of his comrades had stayed in the comfort of Festival. Even Louise with whom he'd gone through three campaigns.

'Just couldn't stay in one place, I guess. Just had to keep on keepin' on.'

That was it. After the first month in Festival he had become restless, split with Lou and signed on to collect a puller for the yards in the North. There he had met old Mac and they had been partners ever since, hauling cara-vans. Mac driving a puller, Eddie either stoking or, eventu-ally, riding herd on the whole deal as wagonmaster. For twenty years they had pushed loads from the Great Bridge, in and out of Festival, to and from the southern ports. He could never settle down. Settling down was a form of dying.

Eddie swung his legs over the side of the bunk. He couldn't shake the restlessness. He dragged on his boots again and laced them.

'I'm goin' out for a last look round.'

'Okay chief, I'll prob'ly be asleep when you ge' back.'

As Big Eddie walked across the compound formed by the circle of wagons, skirting the men grouped around the fire in the middle, a small nervous man hurried up to him.

'Evenin', wagonmaster.'

Eddie recognised the man as Hoover, a small-time crystal dealer travelling alone with a package of crystal in the caravan strong box. The man stretched his face into what Eddie assumed was intended to be an ingratiating smile but which in fact caused him to resemble a lizard. The resemblance was heightened by the way his small body was hunched into his long green coat.

'I trust everything is goin' well.'

Paranoid little shit, thought Eddie.

'Just fine, Mister Hoover, just fine.' Eddie tried to walk off but the little man still seemed to want something.

'How many more days do you think we should be out, wagonmaster?'

'Well, Mister Hoover, we cross Ruined Hill tomorrow an' after that I reckon two days of easy ridin' clear through to Festival.'

'You don't expect any trouble?'

'Well, the piston on the puller is a bit fouled up but I don't think it's ...'

'No, no, wagonmaster, I meaned with bandits, tha' kinda trouble.'

'I don't think so, Mister Hoover, I think you'll find that any serious danger finished when Joe Starkweather breaked the tribes in his last campaign.'

'Sometimes I think Starkweather's greatest success was his publicity campaign.'

Eddie clenched his broad calloused fist. He ought to take the little punk's head off. Then he remembered where he was and how punching out passengers was a sure way to end up right back stoking.

'It takes all kinds of opinions, comrade Hoover.'

At the old commune form of address the little man started, mumbled goodnight and hurried off.

Eddie made his round of the guards and then headed back to the puller to prepare for sleep.

*   *   *

In the grey pre-dawn, Eddie hustled about in the caravan, rousting out his men, yelling for the skinners to get their teams in line and shepherding passengers back onto the wagons.

Hoover the dealer kept out of his way.

When finally he had the caravan strung out into one single line he climbed onto the footplate of the big puller, the giant steam engine that hauled the two biggest wagons. When Eddie had started hauling caravans it had been common for a train to include three or four pullers. Now the rule seemed to be one on each train, with the other wagons being pulled by mule teams.

While the caravan formed up Mac and Danny had fired the boiler and raised a head of steam. And when Eddie climbed onto the footplate, shouting to be off, his nailed boots crashing on the steel floor, everything was ready for the big machine to start moving.

'Ready to roll, chief?'

'Sure Mac, an' let her roll good, make those skinners work to catch up, okay?'

'Okay chief.'

Mac eased open the main valve and the piston slid forward. The big wheels spun a little and Eddie grabbed a brass handrail as the machine lurched forward.

They quickly picked up speed until the mule skinners were forced to run their teams to keep pace with the steam engine and its load.

The rising sun was reflected in the brass trim of the dull black iron boilers and the brass plate beside the smoke-stack that read:

Alvin the Founder—Brum.

Eddie pulled his peaked cap down over his eyes, and leaned out of the side of the cab, letting his shoulder-length, greasy hair fly in the breeze. His uncertainties of the night before began to fade with the exhilaration of letting the puller run.

Leaving the ground where they had camped, the caravan pulled out onto the great highway which, along with the Bridge, formed the most lasting monument of the men who had built them but perished in the disaster.

Eddie knew that if he ran the caravan that fast for long, the mules would tire and fall back. But a brisk start in the morning was refreshing and for a while he leaned on the cab rail, his weed pipe clenched in his teeth. As he expected, a gap was opening between the steam wagons and the first mule team and he signalled to Mac to cut the throttle and match speed with the mules.

The fun of the day was over and it was just a matter of following the highway at the speed of a man running. The three leaned on the rail, letting the breeze offset some of the heat from the firebox that was already darkening their overalls with sweat.

*   *   *

Iggy sat on his horse, hitting crystal and feeling pleased. The meeting between his boys and the barbarians had gone off without serious incident. The overnight camp had resulted in one of his men knifing a tribesman but Winston had shot the man and Oltha wasn't making any trouble, so at present everything was working out very well.

Iggy's girlish face, framed by his wide-brimmed hat and long, curling black hair, was brought to unpleasant life by a slight smirk as he watched Winston setting out his men for the ambush. His grin broadened as he remembered how the hicks' eyes had popped out of their heads when the battle wagons had been rolled out, with their four-horse teams, driver and the six guns behind their steel shields and overhead leather canopy. He had noticed the great degree of respect with which Oltha treated him since the chief had seen Iggy's entire force made ready to fight.

Iggy was still grinning when Oltha rode up on his short-legged pony.

'Hey, hey, buddy, how's things?'

Oltha halted.

'A good, good ambush.'

Sure it's a good ambush, thought Iggy, I spent a long time figuring it. Ruined Hill was a high escarpment with a long, even climb on one side and a steep drop on the other. The caravan would sweat their way up the hill, through the deserted town from which the hill got its name, every minute half expecting bandits to jump them from the overgrown ruins. They'd reach the top with a sense of relief and start to roll down the highway that sharply traversed the face of the scarp.

When they were rolling too fast to stop, the horsemen would break from the woods at the top of the hill and attack them on the run. At the foot of the hill a short upgrade would break the caravan's speed and the archers could go into action. At that point the wagonmaster could do nothing except pull his wagons into a loose protective circle. Then his battle wagons could go in, followed by Oltha's foot men and it would be all over. It was a neat ambush and

36

Iggy knew the hill chief was aware of the fact.

'Your men in position?'

'My men are ready.'

'Scouts're down the road a piece. Nothin' to do but wait.'

'I go join the horsemen.'

'I reckon I'll stay here a while. Till the scouts come in. Then I'll join ya.'

Oltha turned his pony and rode off in the direction of the woods.

Iggy fingered his gun, flicked the reins, and flexed his fingers, watching his rings sparkle in the sunlight. The crystal and the excitement were beginning to get to him. The waiting was hard; he'd better ease off on crystal until the scouts returned. He pulled on his thin black gloves.

Winston rode up and told him everything was ready.

'How're the hill boys makin' out?'

'Fine man, they may be dumb, but they're pros.'

'Ri' on, head for the woods and I'll come in with the scouts.'

Winston rode off, leaving Iggy alone on the sunny hillside. To all appearances it was now deserted save for a single rider on a large black horse.

Iggy sat peering into the hazy distance. Where was the mutherin' caravan?

V

It was a fine morning and Joe Starkweather was walking, taking the air, watching life in the town of Festival. Many men of his age would have been content to sit home and watch life go past but Joe Starkweather was not many men. He knew he stood apart from the majority of people, separated by the Starkweather legend, the spurious myth that was remembered while the ideals that had created the legend were forgotten. To most of them he was just a tall grey-haired man in a leather campaign coat and riding boots, whom they respected because they had always respected him. That seemed to be the way of Festival, the way of humanity. It was reflected all the way from the wild-eyed crystal freaks to textkeepers who bickered about the literal interpretation of words and phrases, and waited for a revelation that would save civilisation, without even a clear concept of what civilisation might mean.

Starkweather limped along the high stone wall. The wall that sheltered the privileged from Common Festival, the sanctuary of the lords, the textkeepers and élite protected by their military. Unwittingly it had been Starkweather himself who had created that military.

He paused at the south-west corner of the wall and stared out over the sprawling city. Immediately beneath him was the Merchants' Quarter, sheltered by its own walls: a solid wooden stockade which was protected by its own guards and retainers. Beside its tents and buildings, the flags of the various craft guilds and traders, with their individual symbols, fluttered in the breeze. Beyond the south wall of the Merchants' Quarter ran the Drag, with its thieves, whores and gamblers. In the morning sunlight its gaudy facias looked cheap and tawdry. Many of his people had joined the merchants, the guards or the hustlers on the

38

Drag: the whole spectrum of human behaviour that the founders of the commune had worked to make a thing of the past. Yet the work of the founders had come to nothing.

Along beside him, with the morning sun just clearing the top of its high canopy, was the enormous structure of the Stage, the focus of authority and culture in Festival. The actual Stage level was some twenty feet off the ground, with the superstructure that had once held banks of speakers and electric lights, and the great plastic canopy. Originally the Stage had been enclosed in wooden side walls, like a barn with one side missing, but over the years all but the boards of the Stage itself had been removed for other buildings, and now only the spidery structure of black rusted iron scaffolding remained. To Joe the Stage represented Festival as a whole, a skeleton that would not concede that its purpose was long dead.

In his youth things had been different. He had grown to manhood in the Western Commune, a busy healthy community organised in the spirit of the text and the writings of the legendary, pre-disaster heroes. He remembered the great names Mao, Huey, Guevara, Angela and Brother John, and the way life in the commune had run on lines of open equality; how they had tackled the problems of reconstructing a culture out of the chaos left behind after the death of the great civilisation.

Of course life had been hard; the ruined soil and poisoned rivers didn't yield a lot to live on but, little by little, they had managed to bring life back to the tainted land. Then the conflicts of the outside world had begun to threaten their work, and Joe had been elected to lead the people's army against the savage tribes who had grown from the greaser gangs that had survived through the disaster years.

The sadness had begun when he had returned from the final campaign. His victorious men and women had returned from the October battle to find the commune fallen into decay. Dogmatism had replaced enlightenment, and the wisdom of the old writings was ignored in a fury of blind worship for the memory of the writers. Reluctantly he had offered his army the choice of staying in the commune, with its narrow code and ideological witch hunts, or following him to find some kind of free life. Most had followed and the commune had closed its doors on the outside world and become a tight, isolated community. Eventually Starkweather and his people had drifted to Festival and had been absorbed by it. The lords had welcomed him; he had organised its military. The years of peace had made him soft. An ageing, half forgotten hero who clung to a few neglected principles that would probably die with him.

Joe limped along the south wall. The pain in his damaged leg decreased in the morning sun. In front of him, beside the Arena Gate, a group of courtiers craned over the wall, laughing and shouting, obviously amused by some spectacle taking place at the foot of the wall.

Joe leaned over the parapet. It was a merchant punishment; a small fat man was being cut down from a post that had been erected by the base of the wall. To one side, armed retainers guarded four prisoners who were roped together at the neck. Nearer the post a group of merchants, one wearing the fur trimmed silk robes of a justice, stood and watched. A huge retainer with a long whip stood stripped to the waist and waiting for his next victim. The guards holding back the crowd of spectators allowed two to come through and help the fat man away. Another prisoner was dragged forward, this time a young woman. The guards secured her hands in the leather straps fixed high on the post and then slit the back of her dress so it fell around her hips. The merchant in justice robes read something, inaudible to Joe, from a paper. The retainer flicked his whip, as though testing it. As the first blow fell and the girl screamed, Joe turned away and walked off in the direction from which he had come.

Humanity was a long way from the founders' conception of a non-authoritarian society.

*   *   *

Frankie Lee stood in the crowd and watched as Claudette got ten. It was always really bad, what with the crowd, the nobles shouting and laughing on the wall. Frankie winced as another blow fell and Claudette's body twisted and squirmed, tugging against the sweat-stained bands that held her wrists. The crowd always had itself a time when the retainers pulled in a woman, gawping at her hanging from the black polished post, stripped to the waist.

Another blow fell, and Claudette screamed and writhed against the post as the whip left another red weal across the brown skin of her back. Frankie gave thanks for the bystanders who had sworn that he had killed the country boy in self defence. If they hadn't come across he'd be strapped to the post himself, and it wouldn't be only ten he'd be getting. It was too bad about Claudette; she was a fool to try stealing purses from merchants who were still sober.

The last blow fell; Claudette shuddered and sagged against the post. Her head was sunk between her shoulders and her long dark hair hid her face. Frankie Lee pushed through the crowd. The least he could do was to help her back to the Last Chance.

*   *   *

Isaac Feinberg was crouched over his bench in the sound shack to one side of the Stage. He squinted into the interior of the stripped-down amplifier and probed with a screwdriver. Each year more of the equipment disintegrated, and in the not-too-distant future it would no longer be possible to put out any sound from the Stage at all. He hoped he would be already dead by then; he didn't want to be the one to tell the high lord that there would be no more text ceremonies. In the meantime, he would go on trying to patch up the ancient circuitry, pay foragers to hunt down spares, and try to build substitutes for the simpler parts. He knew, though, that it was a losing fight.

The whole thing was ridiculous anyway. At the time

Festival had been founded, the dark years of chaos after the disaster, any weird idea had seemed viable to the tiny percentage who had missed death or mindless idiocy. When Homer, the original lord, had led his troop of survivors out of the drowning ruins of 'Ndunn, the idea of founding a festival modelled on the old legendary Events and the hope that in it, men and women could rediscover the old ways and the best of the old spirit was, to the shattered survivors, no more absurd than many of the other survival schemes that had sprung up after the disaster.

Most of those schemes had failed while Festival had, for some reason, flourished and grown to become a bustling city. As the years had passed, the ideas that Homer had used to encourage his people were taken more and more literally. The celebrations that had taken place in Homer's time had become stylised rituals, the music they had brought from the ruins as a means of enjoyment had gradually been adopted as the divine basis of society. The songs had become the texts, the final appeal for all people in Festival; used as if they were holy relics, containing obscure but divine wisdom.

Feinberg wondered why he bothered coaxing ancient, broken sound gear to go on working, so that the textkeepers and the lords could indulge their obscure foolishness. He was too old to change now. Let them build up their walls, hold their rituals; he'd fix the equipment as long as he could. His father and grandfathers had done it before him, he couldn't give up now. Better to take pride in the absurd role of Soundmanager to the lords of Festival than to have no pride at all.

'Just my foolish pride,' he muttered. They even had a text that covered it. At least he had no son to saddle with the lifelong job of tinkering with failing equipment in the tiny shack high in the supports of the vast spidery structure of the great Stage. He shouted for his apprentice, and the boy appeared in the shack doorway. Feinberg pointed to the stripped amplifier.

'Finish putting this together. I'm goin' to the Last Chance

42

for a brew. Old Joe should be there about now lookin' for a chess game.'

*   *   *

Frankie Lee and Wimp, one on either side, carried the semi-conscious Claudette back to the Last Chance.

Fending off the bar flies who gathered for a closer look, they took her into one of the back rooms where they could lay her on a bed. A kid was despatched to find Madame Lou who would have some kind of salve for Claudette's ravaged back.

'At least,' mumbled Frankie cynically, 'she's got the consolation that she'll make a bundle out of pervies who'll pay to touch her back.'

Madame Lou bustled into the room trailing pendants and draperies. Shooing the two men out of the room, she clucked and started to attend to the girl. Frankie and Wimp went up to the bar and ordered beers. Lazy Henry the bartender brought their drinks and leaned on the bar, as though he wanted to chat.

'Bad scene, Claudette gettin' hersel' hauled in fer ten.'

'Yeah, too bad.'

'You coulda got it yoursel' if that rube hadn't had a gun.'

Frankie didn't want to be reminded of the possible consequences of shooting the country boy. Henry leaned closer to Frankie and dropped his voice.

'I bet she sure wriggled some while she was gettin' it, huh?' Henry winked and nudged Frankie's arm. 'I like to see a punishment, but the boss said I had to watch the bar. I bet her tits were flyin' every direction.'

Frankie tried to ignore the barkeep, but Henry went on with his speculation.

'I woulda really like to ha' seen it, watch her ass a-twistin' about. I met a guy onced who said that some women'll try, actually try to get hauled in 'cos they enjoy it. Enjoy it, you believe that, Frankie boy? Huh? You believe that?'

Frankie motioned to Henry to lean closer. He dropped his voice too, mimicking the barman's insinuating whine.

'You know what I think, Henry ole buddy?'

'What?' Henry looked eager. Frankie raised his voice again suddenly.

'I think you got a fat pervy mouth that you oughta keep shut.'

Henry jumped and shuffled off wiping his hands on his apron and muttering. Wimp laughed.

The swing doors opened, briefly letting in the morning sun to light up the dust and smoke inside the bar. Joe Starkweather came in, his walking stick rapping on the board floor. He made his way to the corner table and Henry hurried over with old Joe's regular beer and shot of root spirit. Frankie Lee watched the old man sip his drink. It was funny how a man who could spend his time drinking with lords should choose to come to the Chance almost every morning. Starkweather looked up and beckoned.

'Hey, Frankie Lee, come over here a minute.'

Frankie walked over to the old man's table.

'Take a seat, boy.' He turned to the bar, 'Hey Henry, bring another beer.' He turned back to Frankie Lee.

'I saw a punishment this morning, a woman gettin' flogged. It wasn't a girl from here?'

'Afraid so. Claudette, sir, she got ten.'

'What was she supposed to have done?'

'Clipped a purse off some merchant john. He got home, found it gone and yelled for the retainers.'

'That's too bad.'

'We just brought her back, like.'

'Is she okay?'

'Sure, Claudette's a tough broad. Madame Lou's with her. Reckon she'll sleep it off.'

Starkweather tossed back the tumbler of spirit, took a sip of beer and leaned back to fill his pipe.

'I heard you killed a man, that true?'

44

'Self defence, sir. I took a pile off this country boy an' he went for his gun. Nothin' else I could do.'

'Still robbin' hicks, Frankie, is there nothing else you can do?'

'It was a straight game, sir. A man's gotta make a livin'. I value my freedom too much to hire on as a merchant's watchdog. Anyways the rube was askin' for it. Like the texts say, one should never be where one does not belong.'

'The devil quoting scripture?'

'It's me name-text, sir?'

'Listen, you better split, I see Isaac Feinberg comin' for his chess game. Take care now.'

'I'll try, sir.'

Frankie Lee went back to the bar as Feinberg sat down at Starkweather's table. Henry bustled over with a tray of drinks and the chess board.

VI

The caravan was only a hundred paces from the crest of Ruined Hill, and Big Eddie began to relax. He felt that the muscles in his neck and arms had become stiff with the tension of the climb; he uncurled his hand from around the rail of the cab, realising he had probably been squeezing it for the entire haul up the gradient. He grinned at Mac.

'Looks like we made it.'

'Sure does boss, those ruins give me the creeps. I was just waitin' for a horde of yellin' savages to come burstin' outta the undergrowth.'

'Maybe we're gettin' too old, Mac, lookin' for trouble behind ev'ry bush.'

The big engine breasted the hill top, and Eddie stared out over the broad valley. Covered with high grass, it was such a contrast to the bare brown hills with their clumps of black, diseased trees. Nothing in sight; it looked like a quiet run right through to Festival.

'Let her run free, Mac, blow out the spooks an' cobwebs.'

Mac knocked the engine out of gear, and it began to pick up speed. Eddie glanced behind, and grinned as he saw the first mule team cross the top of the hill and break into a gallop. The puller was now rolling free down the slope, much faster than it could ever run on the flat under its own power.

A sudden movement on the hillside caught his eye; then he stared in disbelief as a line of horsemen broke out of the woods and raced down the hillside to intercept the puller at some point further down the highway. Eddie felt his stomach turn over; there must be a hundred or more racing down the slope. He leaped to the gun rack, yelling to Mac to reduce speed. Mac yanked on the gear shift and

46

the grate of tortured metal screamed from inside the machine.

'I can't slow 'er, chief, she'll just strip her gears an' strand us at the bottom.'

'Grab a gun, an' get under cover.' Eddie ducked as a bullet ricocheted off the boiler. The leading horsemen had opened fire. There was little doubt that they meant business. More bullets thudded into the side of the cab as the first wave of riders drew level with the engine. Eddie let go with one barrel of his shotgun and one rider, a short burly fellow, his head shaved except for a single scalp-lock, dropped from his horse. Mac and Danny were now firing too but there were screaming horsemen on both sides of the cab, keeping up a steady crossfire that made accurate shooting difficult. Then Danny spun and fell against the steering rods. The engine careered across the highway, ploughing through a group of horsemen. Pushing the wounded stoker to one side, Eddie wrestled with the rods to bring the engine back onto the road.

Shouts and scuffling behind him made Eddie turn his head. Mac was clubbing with his gun butt at a thin, wild-eyed outlaw who clung to the outside of the cab, waving a long knife in his free hand. There was a crunch as Mac brought his clubbed gun down on the tattooed hand gripping the cab rail; then the man fell back and was caught by the enormous rear wheels.

*   *   *

Iggy rode flat out to keep pace with the thundering steamer as it rolled headlong down the slope. Every so often it would swerve, side-swiping one of his men and throwing horse and rider screaming to the road. Iggy pumped bullet after bullet into the cab of the big machine, but the speed of the pursuit made it impossible to shoot accurately. His heart pounded from crystal and excitement, his mouth was dry and his lips were drawn back in an animal grin which tightened to a silent scream as the kill-frenzy took control of him. One of his men, loaded beyond rational thought, had leaped onto the side of the puller and, clinging with one hand, was trying to fight his way into the cab. Iggy laughed as the man became dislodged and was crushed by the iron driving wheels. Iggy let go a burst at his man's opponent who stood for a moment silhouetted in the entrance to the cab.

*   *   *

Eddie stared in horror as, almost in slow motion, Mac clawed at his chest, stumbled and, with a growing patch of blood staining his overalls, fell from the cab. Eddie was alone in the big machine, Mac was dead and Danny was either dead or wounded. For a moment he stood dumbly; then the crash of bullets along the side of the cab snapped him back into action.

He sneaked a look forward and saw that the bottom of the hill was coming up fast; a short rise that would certainly break his speed. Behind him at least one of the mule teams was still running. Maybe there was a chance. If he could pull what was left of the caravan into a circle, they might just make it too costly for the horsemen to overrun them. With one arm steadying the steering rods, he loaded the two guns that were left in the cab. Then he bent down and put a hand inside Danny's shirt. As far as he could tell the kid was dead.

Eddie hauled on the rods to bring the engine round as it began to run uphill and lose speed. Finally it stopped, the length of itself and the two wagons forming an arc that almost blocked the road. Eddie jumped from the cab and dived for cover behind the back wheels. He saw Ira, the guard on the rear wagon, dive from the wagon door and also take cover. The first mule team was almost up to him; Charlie was still driving, although of his partner Eddie could see no sign. He crouched as Charlie ducked under the front of the wagon and released the team. The mules thundered past and Charlie jumped as the wagon smashed into the front of the puller and came to rest.

Eddie stood up and fired both barrels of his shotgun at the pursuing riders as Charlie rolled into the cover of the puller's wheels. The passenger door flew open and half a dozen people spilled out and ran towards where Eddie stood. He quickly reloaded and fired again; two riders went down and the rest retreated some distance up the road.

The second mule team thundered towards him. The driver's box appeared to be empty, although the two guards still clung to the flat roof of the big wagon. As the mules swerved to avoid the obstruction, the wagon swayed onto two wheels and crashed over on its side. The two guards jumped clear and struggled to free the plunging, kicking animals. Eddie ran to the wrecked wagon and wrenched open the passenger door. He leaned inside and helped up the three remaining passengers.

'Run for puller, grab any guns you see!'

Eddie ran to the front of the wrecked wagon and reached into the back of the upended driver's box. The two guards had freed the mules and were zigzagging towards the cover of the puller. One repeating rifle remained in the driver's gun rack together with a half-full ammunition belt. As he turned to follow the guards, an arrow thudded into the side of the box. Then more arrows fell, striking the ground and wagon like deadly rain.

*   *   *

Iggy sat on his horse some way up the hill, relishing the cat and mouse game as his archers pinned down the survivors huddled under the steam engine and the four wagons stranded where the road reached the floor of the valley.

He giggled quietly as the thought struck him that the longer he held up the final assault, the greater the chance that the wagonmaster might try some futile attempt to break out. It would be much more amusing if they tried something. Just sending in Oltha's hillbilly butchers seemed an anticlimax after the rush of the downhill chase.

He noticed Oltha between him and the bowmen, riding purposefully in his direction. Iggy kicked his horse and rode down to meet him.

'What's the trouble chief, you lookin' f' me?'

'Soonly my warriors become restless.'

'Yeah, wha's the hurry? We got all day.'

'We come to fight, not watch.'

'Aw, let the bastards sweat for a while, they can't move.'

'We finish it now.'

'Leave it, we ain't had no fun with 'em as yet.'

'We are men, we fight, we move upon them now – now!'

'Lissen . . .'

'Now.' The chief began to look dangerous. No point in looking for trouble this early. Iggy shrugged.

'Send in the slaughter crew then. I'll use the battle wagons to give coverin' fire if you need it.'

'No need of that, the men become impatient for the rush of the manslayer. We finish it.'

Oltha wheeled his horse and galloped to give the orders to his foot men. Iggy turned round more slowly to where Winston had assembled his men around the two wagons.

'Wha's happenin' chief, why the hangup?'

Iggy halted.

'No hangup ol' buddy. Oltha's a-sendin' in his butcher boys. All we have t' do is wait.'

'We ain't a-goin' in?'

'No point in bein' heroes, just move in easy when they've taken care of business. You take two men an' make sho' nobody else gets the strongbox, ri'? An' detail two guys to pick us the pieces from the dead, an' what might be left in the wagons' gun racks, okay?'

'Sho', Marty an' Gay Dave stick by me, an' Pig an' Rummy, you get the guns.'

*   *   *

The arrows fell, volley after volley, making their unique,

eerie hiss. Eddie pressed himself as far back as possible into the driving box of the upturned wagon. Across from him, he could see the puller's wheels. Were the outlaws going to keep them pinned like this forever? Eddie was tempted to make a run for it. Maybe a suicide dash would be better than letting a psychopath hill chief play with him like this. Then, almost in answer, the arrows stopped. Eddie tensed for the dash back to the engine. For a moment there was silence. Eddie, a gun in each hand, made his dash. Halfway across the space a furious shouting began. Hesitating, Eddie glanced round. Running tribesmen were coming from every direction. Two, one brandishing a knife, the other a long axe, ran round the side of the upturned wagon. Eddie fired one barrel of his shotgun and they went down. Turning, he found a tall rangy hill man with an ugly scar down one cheek between himself and the puller. He rushed Eddie, swinging a double-handed axe. Eddie sidestepped, ducked and chopped him with his gun barrel. The man fell but started to rise again and Eddie finished him with his second barrel.

Then they were everywhere; Eddie threw down the shotgun and fired a rapid burst from the repeater. Out of the corner of his eye he saw Charlie backed up against the engine, wielding his gun butt like a club. The burst of fire cleared a space in front of Eddie for an instant, then the clip was exhausted and the tribesmen pressed towards him. In a momentary flash before he was overwhelmed he saw Hoover running desperately, his green coat flapping like useless wings and, still clutching his hat and travelling bag, pursued by three laughing outlaws.

Then they swamped him and Eddie saw nothing.

*   *   *

Although the men shouted and laughed Nath was aware that most of them shared his mild disappointment. The raid would yield much booty but that was for the tribe. For the individual warrior there had been few scalps and no women.

The only consolation was in the dozen kegs of beer that Funka had discovered undamaged in one of the wagons.

Under the supervision of Oltha, the tribesmen unloaded the loot from the wagons. The strange-eyed horsemen of the new tribe moved through the wreck of the caravan, seizing an item here and another there. They seemed to take no great pleasure in the victory.

Nath shouldered a sack of grain and looked forward to the night of drinking.

*   *   *

Iggy stared at the steam engine. It was magnificent with its black ironwork, its shining polished steel pistons and brass fittings. There were dents in it though and some of the cab's wooden panels had been smashed by gunfire. If only it could be made to work. He turned to Winston.

'Any of the boys know how to work this mutha?'

'I think Banana useda boss a puller before he joined us. Hey, Banana, get ya ass over here.'

Banana, a big muscular negro, sauntered over.

'Whasamatta chief? You wants somethin'?'

'The boss wants to know if you kin get this big mutha rollin'.'

'No sweat if'n it ain't bin busted up in the fight.'

Iggy inspected the machine.

'It don't look busted.' He turned to Banana. 'You reckon it'll roll to Festival?'

'No reason why not, all it'll need is wood.'

'Hey Winston, get a coupla Oltha's axe boys to bust up a wagon, an' Banana, get together, let's see if it works.'

'Sho', chief.' He started to climb into the cab. Winston went off to find Oltha. After another look at the steam engine Iggy followed him.

*   *   *

Night fell and a high keening cut through the silent air.

Although they would later be drinking, the men in Oltha's tribe now sat in a rough circle, a short distance from the wrecked and looted wagons, their voices raised in the solemn chant, the ritual Singing of the Dead.

Iggy's men had lit a fire further up the hill, and they huddled around it uncomfortable and tense with the high, droning chant. Iggy stood a little way off, hugging his cloak around him against the evening chill and gazing across the darkening landscape. Figures of the crystal comedown darted at the edge of his vision. Originally he had been impatient at the chief's refusal to discuss the next move until after the tribe's ritual, but after an hour of the wailing chant he was on edge and had to concentrate to stop the hand that gripped the front of his cloak from shaking.

'We sing. It is down upon the victor. The Song of the Dead cannot remain unsung.'

There was a depth to these tribesmen that made Iggy ill-at-ease. He had not allowed for it. Once they were hooked on crystal, he would feel a lot happier. Then it would be he who decided the tribe's rituals.

Slowly he walked down the hill, his black woollen cloak making him almost invisible in the darkness. He gave a wide berth to the mass of squatting, wailing men, almost as though their fur-wrapped figures were the source of a strange power that he had no wish to approach.

The steam engine loomed big in the night, its brasswork reflecting the flicker of the distant firelight. Iggy took off his glove and laid his hand on the cold, dew-wet iron.

'Oh baby, with you nothing can stop me, nothing.'

VII

There was an almost carnival air as Frankie Lee lounged by the entrance to the Merchants' Quarter and watched the soldier boys ride out of the Highway Gate. A crowd had gathered, and fast to cash in, hawkers, pimps and pickpockets moved through the mass of people, taking care of business. He could even hear the tuneless voice of Blind Larry, the wandering text singer.

'Wanna hear a rare tex' for a token?'

The squad of soldiers was clear of the gate, and riding, doing their best to look grim and purposeful, down the highway to the west.

For cats who lounged around all day and scratched themselves they put on a good show, thought Frankie as the troop, about thirty in all, passed him. The first dozen wore the black surcoats with the device of the high lord, the white circle enclosing an inverted 'Y'. The remainder wore the retainer livery of various merchants and cartels.

'What's all the fuss about?' A bearded man in the costume of an out-of-town merchant turned to Frankie. 'Is this some kinda regular parade?'

'No, man. They're a-gonna check ou' some kinda trouble up the highway, some travellers came back with a tale of a caravan gettin' wiped out.'

The merchant looked anxious.

'That's terrible, I'd planned to ride back to the Bridge in the nex' coupla days.'

'Reckon you'd be wise to wait till these troubles are sorted out.'

'Yeah, I guess so.'

The soldiers were now out of sight, and the crowd began to drift away. Frankie turned to go, but the merchant caught at his sleeve with an embarrassed grin.

'Lissen, uh ... you look like a man of the world an' I ...
uh...'

Shit, thought Frankie, now the rube wants to get laid.
Thinking of the possible percentage, he restrained himself
from laughing at the man.

'Yeah?'

'Well, I was wonderin' if'n you could fix me up with a
bit o' fun, you know what I mean.' The man winked.

Frankie moved away a pace before the rube started
nudging him.

'If you wanna get laid, there're plenty o' chippies on the
Drag.'

'Yeah, I was wonderin' if'n you could connect me with
something', like, you know, a bit ... uh ... unusual.'

Frankie stared at the man and the urge to gross him out
became too strong to ignore.

'I know this hooker who got a floggin' not two days ago,
that'd be pretty, uh, bizarre, huh?' Frankie nudged the
man in the ribs and leered at him. The merchant looked
uncertain. Frankie leered again, showing his teeth.

'It won't cost too much and it'll sure be somethin' to tell
the boys back home. C'mon an' buy me a drink, an' I'll fix
ya up.'

Frankie walked off with the man following.

*   *   *

Valentine, the seventh high lord of Festival, sat in the
informal audience room of the stone palace and eyed the
young woman who sat across the room from him. Normally
the high, echoing room with its hangings, carpets and
upholstered furniture, priceless objects from the days
when men had crossed the sea, the smell of incense and the
girl, painted and dressed solely to be an object of his lust,
would have filled him with a happy sense of what he called
exquisite grandeur. But today his full, rather cruel lips were

thrust into a pout that gave his face the expression of a sullen child.

This trouble on the highway was monstrous. Probably some brain-damaged drifter had made up the tale for drinks and the soldiers would find nothing. There was no excuse for dragging him from his bed and sport so early in the day. The young woman with the gold hair and small firm breasts was excellent, one of the best his agents had ever found, and although he would quickly tire of her the novelty of the new body was still such that it irked him to have to spend the day investigating a fool's paranoid fantasies.

The doors opened and Senior Official Lazarus bowed in. The old man in his long black robes stood silently in front of the door; Valentine was tempted to ignore him, but knew he would probably stand there for ever if he did. For a while Valentine examined the rings on his left hand. Then he raised his head.

'Well?'

'The textkeepers request audience, my lord. Phelge an' Wheatstraw wait without. They claim they have amassed such Self-Evident Truths as can be gleaned from the texts regarding the current emergency.'

Valentine cursed under his breath. After half the morning haggling over who should provide the soldiers for the inspection party, the textsayers now wanted their token's worth. Any advice those two dodderers might offer would be buried in an hour's debate over points of definition. It was unfortunate that his authority and title were so intertwined with the belief in the texts that he was unable to rid himself of the old fools. Personally he viewed the textkeepers' lore as irrelevant nonsense and was sure that when his ancestor Homer the Leader had talked of 'the spirit of Wustock returning to his people', his vision had not included the continuing debate as to why the spirit was depicted in the old prints as a small scruffy bird accompanied by a dog figure in a strange helmet. Nonetheless, he was forced to pay lip service to the absurd cult, since

56

it kept the people quiet and maintained his position.

Valentine brushed imaginary fluff from the sleeve of his velvet tunic and noticed with distaste that the nail polish on his right hand had already begun to chip.

'I s'pose you better show them in, but make it clear that I cannot spend too long with them. Oh, an' after they've left I shall want to eat. Is that clear?'

'Yes, my lord.' Old Lazarus bowed and left the room. A few moments later he returned, followed by the two text-keepers in ceremonial robes. He backed from the audience room, closing the door as he left. The textkeepers bowed in unison and stood looking anxious. Valentine sat for a while watching them.

'Well, what have you got to waste my time with now?'

'My lord, we have studied the texts an' I hope we have searched out those that might apply to the current problem. But, my lord, it is difficult...'

'What is difficult?'

Phelge looked uncomfortable. Will Wheatstraw darted a glance towards the woman.

'My lord, I hesitate.'

Valentine laughed.

'Oh, it's the woman, is it,' he turned to face her, 'you better split, my love, you make these learned brothers uncomfortable.'

The girl stood up and walked towards the door. As she passed Wheatstraw and Phelge she twitched her hips exaggeratedly. Valentine roared with laughter and Phelge turned a similar shade of crimson to his robe.

'My lord, I...'

'Stop shuffling and stammering, you look absurd. Jus' tell me what line of rubbish you intend to feed to the rabble about these supposed bandits.'

'If only my lord could find a greater degree of faith in the blessed texts, it would...'

'Your lord has immense faith in the influence that the texts have on the ignorant and superstitious populace, so come to the point.'

'My lord is prob'ly aware that the subject of violent robbery is a popular theme that recurs throughout the great texts.'

'I was aware; I have heard enough of them.'

'The general trend with this class of texts is that of the eventual triumph of authority, an' I would cite the well known "I fought the law, but the law one" as a primary example although,' he glanced at Wheatstraw who, while still silent, seemed to be controlling an urge to interrupt, 'some of my colleagues who place an illogical store by the A.J. concordance would read far deeper meanings into what is a simple matter of literal symbolism.'

Wheatstraw appeared to burst.

'My lord, I must protest at my brother's...'

'Enough!' Valentine began to get angry. 'I refuse to listen to interminable wrangling over irrelevant points of interpretation.'

'But my lord, when this man takes it upon himself to...'

'Enough!'

The two old men fell silent.

'Good. Now, as I see it, we circulate the idea that the outlaws will get theirs because that is what was written, an' give out a few suitable quotations to back up that idea. I am right?'

'My lord, it is not...'

'Am I right, yes or no?'

'In very basic terms – yes. Except...'

'Well, my lord, there is an obscure text which we have come across; unfortunately both author and title are unknown, but the fragments that remain seem to relate very closely to the situation which we are dealing with.'

'Don't you think we are takin' your precious texts a little too seriously?'

Phelge pressed his lips together in a pious scowl.

'My lord, all matters relating to the...'

'I know, I know, just tell me what it says. I don't need a lecture on my lack of belief.'

'Well, my lord, basically we only have a few lines we can pick out. I had them transcribed from the tape.' He produced a sheet of paper from under his robe. 'They read:

"The outlaws come flying, out of the west,
    On their pale lips are framed words of death",

then there's a break an' it continues:

"Come on everybody, come gather round friends,
    This is the day civilisation ends.
    Let's get together and do death's dance
    And go loot",

the rest of the line is undecipherable. That is all, my lord. It would seem that our own outlaws do in fact "come flying out of the west". We thought it might have some bearing on the problem.'

'It hardly seems conducive to social order and stability. It is my wish that the existence of this text is not made generally known, is that clear?'

'But my lord, surely it constitutes a crime against the purpose of the Leader to deliberately suppress a text?'

'I shall be the judge of that. I am the lord an' I am the embodiment of the Purpose. At the next celebration – what's that? in five days I think – you will broadcast texts on the lines I have indicated. As for your little gem of potential civil disorder – lose it! That is not only my wish, but my order.' Valentine stood up. 'Now leave me. Oh, an' send the woman back in.'

The textkeepers bowed out and Valentine sprawled back in his chair. The girl came in and closed the door behind her. He smiled as she walked towards him.

'Relax me, my dear. Those fools have made me very tense.' Then he closed his eyes as the girl kneeled in front of him and slowly brought her face down to his lap.

*   *   *

Once they were beyond sight of the crowd around the Highway Gate, the troop captain gave the order to relax the brisk parade pace. With no more spectators to impress the whole troop began to relax, the thirty riders broke the formation and the neat column dissolved into a string of horsemen riding in groups of twos and threes.

Billy Joe eased the carbine off his shoulder and laid it across his saddle. He cursed his luck to get picked for a four day fool's errand into the wilderness, just as One-Legged Terry had fixed him up with a hot number. As the sun grew hotter, he stripped off his denim surcoat, with the colours of the Allied Metal Factors across the back, and pulled a jug of beer from his saddle bag. As he pulled the stopper, Hud Daley, the troop captain from the lord's squad, pulled his horse over to fall into step with Billy Joe.

'You wanna pass that brew over here, Billy Joe?'

'Sure captain, here.' Billy Joe passed the jug over. 'How long you think we're gonna be chasin' these said outlaws roun' the boonies?'

'Dunno man. Jus' foolishness if'n you ask me. If'n them outlaws really jumped a caravan they're gonna be long gone by the time we get there. Bes' we can do is ride out to wha's left of it, take a look an' go home.'

'Yeah, how long you reckon all tha's gonna take? I got a thing goin' with One-Legged Terry.'

'I don't aim to stay out more'n five days, mebbe stop over-night in Afghan Promise each way, an' get some laughs. No point in bustin' yer ass.'

'Stay out five days, an' go back an' say the outlaws were long gone?'

The captain grinned.

'I never said that. We gotta "preserve the security of Festival, an' pursue the wrongdoers", th' lord tole me his-self.' He laughed, 'I reckon five days, an' be home for Celebration. One-Legged Terry's lining some little number for me too.'

Billy Joe took another hit on the jug and they rode in

silence. A stopover in Afghan Promise was some consolation; the little commune had grown over the years until it was a wide open highway stop. There'd be a chance for some action tonight after all.

*   *   *

Iggy sat at the chief's table with Oltha and Winston and watched the interminable knife game. One by one the tribesmen had eagerly taken turns to sever their fingers. They had even offered him a place in the line. Iggy had politely declined the invitation.

Since the caravan had been taken the time had begun to drag. Iggy was starting to find life in the makeshift camp more than tedious.

They had loaded the loot from the raid into a wagon, hitched it to the puller and, under the direction of Winston and Banana, they had rolled the machine down a side road for perhaps a mile. Oltha had followed with his men and they had made camp. Messengers had been dispatched to bring in the remainder of the tribe and preparations had started on the next stage of their campaign.

While Banana had worked on the puller Iggy had watched with some interest, but once the machine had been announced as being in perfect working order Iggy had started to become bored. The camp was full of gun-cleaning, knife-sharpening outlaws, and the invitation to Oltha's tent had been an added nuisance, since he had hoped to get some of Oltha's boys into the joys of crystal while they were in camp. The old man seemed to watch his men like a mother hen, and Iggy had found no way to get a few of them some place quiet where he could casually pass round his stash. Then an idea struck him that could be the answer to all his problems.

'Why don' we ride to Afghan Promise, take a few of the boys an' check it out?'

Winston turned from watching the game.

'How long befo' the resta the hillbillies arrive?'

61

'Dunno; two, three days, plenty of time to get there an' back, an' have us a time.'

'Sounds good to me; how 'bout the chief? We leave him in charge?'

Iggy leaned over to Oltha.

'Ya ever bin t' Afghan Promise?'

'We have never before come this close to Festival.'

'It's the only town 'tween here an' Festival. I was thinkin' it might be worth a visit.'

The chief looked surprised.

'Another raid so soonly?'

'No, no chief, not a raid; jus' ride into town, have a buncha drink, look the place over an' split. Plenty of heavy cats there, we take mebbe a dozen boys, we'll jus' look like travellers. They'll think we're hired guns lookin' fer a gig.'

'I have much to do here.'

'Yeah, I thought I might take Winston an' some o' the boys. Mebbe you should send a coupla your boys so they kin report back, you dig?'

Oltha looked thoughtful.

'It seems like a good plan.'

Iggy smiled. The suspicious old goat had swallowed it.

'Sho' it's a good plan, we'll know the layout befo' we hit them.'

'When do you go there?'

'No time like now, I'll leave Banana in charge o' my boys an' we'll head out. If we ride tonight we kin get there by the afternoon, an' mebbe get back by late the day after, 'bout the time your people show.'

'Sounds good.'

Iggy glanced sideways at the chief.

'How many of your boys you gonna send?'

'I send Nath, and the brothers Rodo and Ona.'

The game stopped and the three tribesmen stood up at Oltha's signal.

'You ride with Iggy tonight, he is to be obeyed as a chief. Go with him.'

The three tribesmen looked at Iggy and nodded.

Perfect, thought Iggy, they've fallen right in. He turned to Winston.

'Pick four or five good boys an' tell 'em to get the horses.'

He turned to the three tribesmen.

'Get your ponies an' meet us by the fire outside.'

They all bid formal farewell to Oltha who stood up as they ducked out of the tent flap.

VIII

Eggs Akerly's joint was full of drunken soldiers. Iggy stopped dead inside the doorway. He had run from soldiers enough times to have an instant reaction to the sight of sleeveless surcoats.

He pulled himself together and pushed his way through the crowd, followed by Winston and one of the tribesmen. He leaned close to Winston and dropped his voice.

'Ya got the script we took off the bodies?'

'Sho'.'

'Gimme some.'

Winston reached in his pouch and handed Iggy a handful of script.

'Here.'

'Thanks, now score some spirits an' I'll get a table.' Iggy shouldered his way through the crowd towards a corner table.

There sure were a lot of soldiers, he thought. Afghan Promise had no army of its own; it was only a strip of fun houses and a few shacks along the side of the main highway, a pull-in where travellers a day out from Festival could stop, get drunk and sport with the whores. Looking round he calculated there must be over two dozen troopers. What were a bunch of Festival soldiers doing this far out? They usually stuck close to the city. Unless, he grinned as the thought struck him, they were looking for him. A search party for the caravan robbers.

Winston and Nath came through the crowd. Winston was carrying two jugs. They sat down.

Iggy stared round the room. None of the soldiers were looking at them; most seemed too drunk to care about anything but the bar girls. Iggy took a hit of crystal and a swallow of the hard corn spirit. He hoped the other boys were making out okay in the other joints along the strip. It was fortunate that they hadn't arrived until after dark. If the soldiers were looking for them, it might have aroused suspicion if they had ridden in in broad daylight.

'Lotta soljas in here, chief,' Winston glanced round the room. Nath's tribesmen looked uneasy in the presence of so many Festival men.

'I'd really like to know what they're doin' here.'

Iggy took another mouthful of spirit.

'Bes' way to find out's to ask.'

Two bar girls swayed past, Nath stared at their tight dresses and slit skirts and swallowed quickly. Iggy laughed and beckoned them over. They gave out the standard come-on.

'You wanna good time, boys?'

'Siddown an' have a drink, we wanna talk with you.'

'We're workin' girls mister, time's money.'

Iggy slapped a paper on the table.

'Siddown!'

'Anything you say, mister.'

The two girls sat down, displaying cleavage and thighs. Nath looked as though his collar was too small. Iggy passed them a jug.

'Lotta soljas in town?'

'Sure, cheap bastards from Festival, want a reduction on everything. Claim they're savin' us from outlaws.'

'Outlaws?' Iggy pretended to look surprised. 'Sho' are a lotta soljas for one buncha outlaws.'

'Ain't you heard, dear? A caravan was turned over at Ruined Hill, they're gonna get whoever done it.'

'No kiddin'?'

'You never heard about it, on the road?' The girl looked suspicious.

'We been in the hills.'

'Oh.' The girl lost interest and took a swallow from the jug and crossed her legs.

'I don' wanna hustle you, dear, but did you want us for somethin'?'

65

Iggy looked at the round-eyed Nath and smiled slowly.

'One of yous could take care o' my buddy here. He's a country boy an' he ain't too smart, but I'm sho',' he laid two more papers on the table, 'one o' yous could improve his education.'

The second girl stood up.

'C'mon then country boy, let's go have a time.' Nath scrambled to his feet and the girl led him towards the back door. Quickly Iggy called her back and pushed two more bills into the front of her dress.

'Make sho' he has hisself some crystal; know what I mean?'

The girl winked knowingly.

'Sure.'

He turned to Winston as Nath and the girl left the bar.

'We better move the party in here, case of trouble. Go round up the boys an' send 'em in here. Meantime I'll talk to this here young lady.'

Winston got up and went to round up the men; Iggy looked at the girl.

'You ever had a cat who was, like, into a lotta crystal?'

The girl looked hard at him and nodded.

'Then you'll know about their, uh, special requirements.'

*   *   *

Billy Joe was drunk. He was dimly aware that most of his buddies were as drunk as he was. They had reached Afghan Promise just as the sun was setting, stabled the horses, headed for Eggs's joint and got down to serious drinking. Some of the boys were out in the back tumbling with the bar girls, but most were crowded round the bar, laughing, shouting and singing.

The room started to spin and Billy Joe staggered towards the main door of the bar. Out on the front porch of the bar he leaned against a post and was violently sick, and then clung there, taking deep breaths and hoping the night air would clear his head. He heard the click of heels and raised his head to see the blurred image of a girl coming towards him.

'You all right, mister?'

'Sure baby,' Billy Joe pushed himself away from the post and stood swaying, 'how's about you'n'me goin' in back, an' you'll see jus' how all right I am.'

'You got any money, solja? You gotta pay for your fun.'

Billy Joe grinned drunkenly.

'You ain't gonna charge me, are you darlin'?' He lurched towards her. 'I'm savin' you from them baby-eatin' outlaws.'

The girl sidestepped and he sprawled against the wall. Swinging her hips, she walked back into the bar, leaving Billy Joe clutching the wall and struggling to stand upright.

'Come back here you bitch. Come back here an' I'll teach you some fuggin' manners.'

Billy Joe staggered inside the bar and looked round. The room appeared to swirl about him and he fought to keep his balance. He couldn't see the woman anywhere and sat down heavily in a handy chair. The room spun and his head, cradled in his arms, rested on the table. For a while he shut his eyes but that seemed to make things worse. He opened them again and stared into a blurred mid-distance.

He remained motionless for what seemed like a long while. A part of the blur connected with his dulled consciousness as being in some way familiar. With some difficulty he focused his eyes. The woman! The one with the long legs and black straight hair. He'd been longing to get those legs wrapped around his waist and now the bitch was over there, sitting at a table with some drifter. To make it worse, the drifter looked like a faggot.

Billy Joe raised his head and muttered beneath his breath. Then, swaying, he climbed to his feet.

'Godam whore, leavin' honest soljas thuh to...'

He lurched, and grabbed at a table to steady himself. Few heads turned; it was just another drunk mumbling to himself.

'Godam whore!'

Still she ignored him, laughing with the drifter, and drinking from his jug. Billy Joe raised his voice.

'GODAM WHORE!!'

The bar room became quiet, and the captain stood up and moved towards him.

'You've had too much, Billy Joe, c'mon now.'

Billy Joe pushed past him and lurched to the table where the woman and the drifter sat.

'Wha' you doin' wiv me woman, mufug?'

Iggy looked up as the drunken soldier staggered towards him. He placed both his gloved hands flat on the table, watching the man intently.

'One of you soljas, take this bum away befo' he gets hurt.'

With a snarl Billy Joe had grabbed for Iggy's throat but one of Iggy's hands shot out and chopped Billy Joe under the jaw. He sprawled backwards on the floor, shaking his head and pulling his knife from his belt. Knife in hand he moved more cautiously towards Iggy who edged sideways, away from the table.

'It's yer las' warnin' solja.'

'I'm gonna cut yer ...'

Before Billy Joe could finish the sentence, Iggy had a gun in his hand.

The shot hit Billy in the stomach; he folded in half, his legs gave way and he hit the floor.

When Winston returned to Eggs Akerly's with the rest of the men, the place seemed unnaturally quiet. Then he heard a shot and Iggy's voice shouting 'Hold it'. He slipped the repeater from his shoulder, and broke into a run. As he burst through the door, Iggy was backed, gun out, against the wall and a group of five soldiers were advancing on him. Winston fired a burst into them and Iggy dived for the floor, letting go two shots as he dropped.

The rest of the Festival men milled drunkenly, reaching for discarded weapons and struggling to rise. Nath burst through the back door, holding his gun with one hand and his shirt in the other. One of the soldiers raised his gun but Winston fired another burst that cut him down, along with two of his fellows.

Iggy yelled 'Split', and he and Nath made a break for the door, firing as they ran. Winston paused for them to get clear, then fired a quick burst as he backed out of the door.

As the outlaws ran for the stables, soldiers milled out of the bar and bullets made angry humming sounds as they fired after them. Iggy swung round and returned their shots.

Then they were mounted and the night swallowed them as they raced out of town.

*   *   *

After two days and a night Hud Daley was sick and angry. Angry at the way he had let his men get so drunk that they could be taken like children; angry at the outlaws who had gunned down nine of his men; and angry that after tracking them for a day and a night he and his remaining men had finally lost them. His eyes were red with fatigue, he hadn't shaved and most of the men looked as bad as he did. At the very least he would be busted back to trooper, and would probably be lucky to escape a flogging when he returned to Festival with only two thirds of his original squad. After an afternoon's fruitless searching, there was nothing left to do but give the order to take the trail back to the highway.

The setting sun threw the trail into deep shadow as it wound between two low ridges. Preoccupied with his own failure Daley did not notice the movement on the ridge between him and the sun. Only when the man in front of him screamed and tugged at the arrow buried in his throat, did he realise that he was under attack.

Another man, and then another, dropped from their saddles. Daley fired wildly into the dazzling sun as rifle shots rang out, adding bullets to the steady stream of arrows.

Suddenly his horse collapsed under him and he was

thrown to the ground. He rolled to avoid the hooves of the thrashing horse, and scrambled to his feet. Crouching he ran to where some of his men were firing at the ridge, squinting into the sun in an attempt to locate their invisible attackers.

Halfway there, he was spun round as a bullet tore into his shoulder. The ground tilted and it was suddenly black.

*   *   *

Iggy ordered his men to keep firing until nothing moved in the little valley. Then cautiously they rose from cover and advanced slowly down the slope. At the bottom they halted, and looked around at the litter of dead men and horses. Iggy walked among the carnage: nothing moved; the slaughter seemed complete. Then out of the corner of his eye Iggy saw the captain of the troop raise his head. Iggy stood still and grinned as the man painfully tried to raise his rifle. For a moment he held it poised and then, before he could pull the trigger, slumped as his strength gave out.

Still grinning, Iggy walked over to where the man lay, and put a bullet in the back of his head.

'There, solja boy. You sho' found your outlaws.'

IX

Blind Larry shuffled down the Drag in the grey dawn, his cane tapping in front of him finding a safe path in the pot-holed and rutted avenue. The rustle of windblown garbage and the creaking of a swinging bar sign provided a coarse background as he murmured to himself and sang softly:

> 'Come on everybody,
> Come gather round friends.'

A dog trotted quickly down the avenue, on furtive dog business, giving the muttering blind man a wide berth.

> 'This is the day
> Civilisation ends.'

A sleepy figure, huddled by the wall of Madame Lou's, stirred slightly as Blind Larry went by, then drawing its legs closer to its chest it continued its unhappy sleep.

> 'Let's get together
> And do death's dance.'

His foot struck an empty spirit bottle and he bent down, feeling with his hand, to pick it up. Hooking his cane over his arm, he raised the jug to his lips to drink any discarded trickle. Nothing came and he hurled the bottle across the avenue. The dog barked as it rattled off the sidewalk in front of Cindy's Pleasure Parlour. Blind Larry spat in the dust and shuffled on.

The crash of swing doors from the direction of the Last Chance made him stop singing and pause to listen attentively.

On the sidewalk in front of the Last Chance, Frankie Lee yawned and stretched. It had been a good night's game despite the fact that he had come out with little more than he had sat down with. An honest game among professionals was much more satisfying than just taking money off a mark.

Seeing the blind man standing in the middle of the avenue, he called out to him.

'Hey Larry, wha's 'appenin'?'

The blind man stared sightlessly in the direction of the voice.

'Who's 'at, who's talkin'?'

'It's me, Larry, Frankie. Frankie Lee the Gambler.'

The old man stood still, saying nothing. His ragged coat flapped in the breeze. Frankie Lee stepped off the sidewalk.

'Well Larry, ain't you got nothin' to say? Wha's the word, ol' man?'

'Wha's the word, Frankie Lee the Gambler, named for the text? I have no word. What word? Word for what?'

Frankie Lee grinned; the old man was crazy, but he had the gift of fools.

'No word for this new morning in Festival, Celebration morning?'

'No word for Celebration, no word for morning, but for Festival there is a word in the west, too soon to know, p'raps the pale word, p'raps death.'

'Death, ol' man? Or mebbe weed an' corn spirit. Let's knock up Madame Lou, mebbe she'll serve us eggs. Words of death run before a full gut.'

Frankie Lee clapped Blind Larry on the shoulder and led him off in the direction of Madame Lou's.

*   *   *

Joe Starkweather slung his legs over the side of the bed and fumbled with his weed pouch. Lighting his pipe he inhaled deeply and coughed. There was little point in trying to sleep any longer; his leg had hurt like hell all night, and now that the dawn was filtering through the window shutters there was little use in a pretence of rest. He would be better occupied watching the early preparations for Celebration.

He pulled his shirt over his head, struggled painfully into his hide pants, and pulled on his boots. Then, throwing his coat over his shoulders, he limped out of his quarters.

The paved courtyard of the walled Backstage was deserted except for a cat that prowled through the previous night's garbage. Starkweather headed across the yard in the direction of the guard house beside the Highway Gate.

He rapped on the heavy wooden door and after some delay a trooper, rubbing his eyes and straightening his surcoat and belt, opened it.

'Joe Starkweather! You're about early.'

'Couldn't sleep, Luther. Ain't you gonna let me in?'

'Sure, sure. C'mon in.'

Luther held the door as Starkweather walked into the guard house and then shut it behind him.

'Sit down, wanna drink?'

'Sure, why not.'

Starkweather seated himself at the square wooden table. Luther brought mugs and a bottle of spirit. Two more troopers lay asleep in a double bunk against the wall. Luther splashed corn spirit into the mugs, and raised one to his lips.

'Cheers Joe.'

'Yeah, cheers.' Starkweather picked up his mug and drank. Then he set it down and looked at the soldier.

'So tell me Luther, how are things?'

'Much as usual.'

'Yeah. Hud Daley back with that patrol yet?'

'Not yet.'

'I'd have thought he'd be back by now.'

'I reckon he'll ride in today. I don't see him chasin' round the hills longer than he needs to.'

'Unless he found some real outlaws.'

'Come on, Joe, outlaws would've been long gone by the time Hud got there.'

'Maybe. Any outlaw who's prepared to jump a big caravan

73

that close to Festival must be pretty confident, perhaps have something to be confident about.'

'Could just be crazy.'

'I just reckon any outlaws who could take on a caravan could give Hud an' his patrol a hard time.'

'Lissen Joe, I reckon today'll see Hud an' his boys ridin' in. If not today, tomorrow at the latest.'

'Yeah, you're most likely right.'

Luther refilled the mug and they both drank. The hard liquor temporarily eased Joe's sense of misgiving and for a while they sat in silence. Joe filled his pipe and passed his pouch to Luther. Just as he was about to light up, there was a rap on the door. Luther stood up and slid back the bolt. A trooper waited outside.

'Whassamatta Mose, you're s'posed to be at the gate.'

'I know Luther, but I jus' heard something from a weed buyer who jus' rode in from Afghan Promise that I thought I oughta come over an' tell you.'

'Okay, okay, what is it?'

'Well, it seems that this fella was in Eggs's joint in Afghan Promise a few nights ago, an' Hud an' his boys come in there an' start drinkin' it up. Way I reckon, it musta been their first night out. Anyhow, it seems one of them gets in a fight with some drifter over a chippy, an' then the drifter's partners show up an' shoot the place up. Anyway, like them drifters waste a buncha Hud's boys an' split an' Hud takes off after them soon as his boys are sober enough t' ride.'

Luther and Starkweather looked at each other, then Luther turned back to the soldier.

'Did this guy say how many men Hud lost?'

'He didn't rightly know, but he figured it musta been around seven, mebbe eight or nine.'

'An' the outlaws got away?'

'Yeah, seems Hud's boys were really ripped, an' at least one of these guys had a rapid-fire.'

Luther turned to Starkweather.

'What are drifters doin' with rapid-fire guns?'

74

Starkweather frowned but said nothing. Luther turned back to the trooper.

'Lissen Mose, you go back to the gate an' find out all you can, but keep your mouth shut until we have more information.'

Mose returned to his post and Luther shut the door after him. Starkweather sat down looking thoughtful. For a while he stared at the table. Then he looked up.

'Maybe I'm gettin' old an' paranoid, but I just get a vibe of trouble. Real trouble. Outlaws with rapid-fires, an' looted caravans on the main highway, it's like somethin' was brewin' in the hills.'

'I dunno Joe. I jus' know the lord's gonna freak out all over the guy who tells him a buncha his boys have been wasted.'

Joe shrugged.

'That's Festival, what can you do? Somebody's gonna have to tell him.'

'Yeah, but I sure wish it wasn't down to me.'

*   *   *

Valentine lay entwined with his two women of the previous night. His make-up was smeared and the bedchamber was littered with discarded jugs, broken glass and scattered rugs and cushions. On the floor beside them an overturned silver box spilled crystal onto the carpet. Torn and strewn clothing added further indication of the strenuous evening.

A rapping on the door caused him to stir and turn over. One of the women awoke.

The rapping was repeated. She sighed and sat up.

'Our lord's asleep,' she hissed, 'go away.'

The voice of a servant came from beyond the door.

'My lord must prepare for Celebration.'

The girl turned to Valentine and, stroking his hair, whispered to him.

'My lord.'

Valentine rolled over and buried his face in a pillow.

75

'Let me sleep, damn you.'

'But my lord...'

'Leave me alone or I'll have you on the stake.'

The girl crouched back among the cushions and kept silent while the knocking on the door was repeated. Valentine sat up.

'Go away, fug you, or I'll have the skin off your back.'

'But my lord, Celebration, my lord. You gave orders to be awakened.'

Valentine stood up and wrapped a robe around himself. Throwing the door open he seized the servant by the front of his tunic.

'Who told you to come disturbing my sleep?'

'Lazarus, my lord.'

The man stammered, wide-eyed with fright. Valentine suddenly released him, and he staggered back into the corridor.

'Fetch me beer and a fresh box of crystal, an' don't hang about or you'll regret it. And send Lazarus up here.'

The servant scuttled away, and Valentine turned back into the room where the two naked girls sat nervously in the big bed. He waved his hand towards the door.

'Out! Take your clothes an' get back to the Drag or wherever it is you were brought from.'

The girls hastily squirmed into their clothes and hurried from the room, passing Lazarus who came in with a tray in one hand and a freshly pressed suit of clothes over his arm.

'I've brought your clothes, my lord, a jug of cold beer, an' a box of crystal.'

Valentine grunted.

'What kinda day is it?'

'The sun is up, my lord, an' it looks as though it might be fine.'

Valentine sat down and swallowed a draught of beer. He took a generous hit of crystal and shook his head.

'My mouth tastes like a sanitation pit.'

'Is there anything else I can get you, my lord?'

'No! Just shut your mouth an' help me dress. Did you bring the black satin?'

Half an hour later Valentine, in his ceremonial satin tunic and trousers and high leather boots, strode into the formal audience room where the textkeepers and officers of the guard waited for him, bowing as he entered.

'He sent word that he would be here shortly, he is makin'

'Is Feinberg here?'

Wheatstraw, the senior textkeeper, bowed.

'He sent word that he would be here shortly; he is makin' adjustments to the equipment balance.'

Valentine scowled and sat down.

'His belief that he is irreplaceable is making him insolent. You,' he pointed at a guard, 'go fetch the old fool.'

Before the guard could comply, the door opened and Isaac Feinberg bustled in. He smiled benignly round the assembly.

'I think the equipment should work okay, maybe even the after-dark lights.'

Valentine pursed his lips.

'I'm so glad you're finally satisfied, Mister Feinberg.'

Feinberg appeared not to notice the sarcasm and beamed all the more.

'Thank you, my lord.'

Valentine stood up.

'If this tedious performance is to start on time, I suggest we should move to the Stage, now Mister Feinberg has condescended to join us.'

The guards came to attention and the courtiers divided, leaving a clear path to the door; then they fell in behind him as he left the room.

*   *   *

The crowds had been converging on Festival since just after dawn and by just before noon a crowd of nearly ten thousand was packed into Festival's broad arena.

Frankie Lee moved through the crowds, catching snatches

of conversation and drinking in the hustling atmosphere. Everywhere he went the main topic seemed to be the missing caravan and the Afghan Promise shootout. He heard Blind Larry's strange text repeated and there seemed an extra quality of tension present among the crowd.

None of it seemed to deter the hawkers, beer vendors, whores or pickpockets who did the roaring trade expected at Celebration. Frankie even saw Blind Larry himself, shuffling through the crowd, offering his texts to the waiting throng.

Then the ancient sound system hummed and crackled as power was fed into it. Frankie began to work his way to the front for the best possible view.

*   *   *

'My lord, the power is running an' everything is ready.'

Lazarus stood respectfully beside Valentine as Festival society milled in the Backstage refreshment hall, and servants circulated bearing wine and quartered chickens. Valentine, camp-sinister in black satin, held a glass of wine in one hand while with the other he fondled a young woman whose red velvet cape was thrown back to reveal the elaborate designs on her breasts and torso painted in vivid colours that contrasted with her wide, white studded belt and long matching boots.

Valentine turned to face the old Official.

'Are you telling me that I'm keeping the mob waiting?'

'Of course not, my lord. It's just that...'

'It's just that you're trying to hustle me into the private enclosure.'

He looked a the girl.

'I don't think this old fool will give me any peace until I take my seat. Shall we go, my dear?'

The girl lowered her eyes.

'Whatever you wish, my lord.'

Valentine turned towards the Stage entrance, but stopped as he saw Joe Starkweather hurrying towards him. Valen-

78

tine cursed under his breath. Starkweather was the one man who made him nervous. If it wasn't for the ridiculous affection that the mob had for the man, he would have disposed of Starkweather years earlier.

'Ah, Joe Starkweather. You don't usually attend a Celebration; I thought you boasted little enthusiasm for our simple beliefs?'

Starkweather smiled.

'I've nothing against a pantomime, Lord Valentine. In any case, I needed to speak to you.'

'I'm just on my way to the enclosure...'

Starkweather cut him short.

'This won't take a moment. There's a guard captain outside who has what I consider vital information.'

'I don't think it could be anything that won't wait until this evening.'

Valentine turned on his heel and hurried from the hall before Starkweather could reply.

*　　　*　　　*

'No rain.'
　'No rain!'
　'No rain.'
　'No rain!'

A junior textkeeper led the crowd in the traditional chant for good weather. The sound system broke into a distorted roar and the crowd cheered the start of the first text.

As the introduction pounded away, four mummers danced onto the Stage carrying their carved instruments, faithful replicas of those in oldtime prints, and wearing the huge grotesque masks, each representing an Author. The voice cut through the blur of electric sound.

> 'Unermathum thersagirl
> whonce hadme down.'

A fifth figure capered onto the Stage in the mask of the legendary Djeggar, the witch king of before the disaster.

79

A ripple went through the crowd as the figure pranced, hand on hip. There were few in the crowd who hadn't been threatened as tiny children with the figure of evil who would 'stick his knife right down your throat'.

Group after group of mummers performed on the wide Stage until, just before sunset, a reverent hush fell across the arena as a single figure in a mask with heavily-sunken cheeks, a thin jutting nose and a mass of black curly wig walked slowly to the front of the Stage, and the first of the Great Texts was played.

The symbolic figure of the prophet Dhillon swayed gently as the texts crackled from the ancient speakers. Finally, when the sun had gone down and the holy lights had blossomed into their electric brilliance, the sound faded and the figure walked from the Stage. The crowd shuffled restlessly, anxious to be away to the traditional night of revelry, but aware that until the lord had completed the announcements, there would be no drink served in Festival.

A line of soldiers filed onto the Stage and took up positions at the rear. The senior textkeepers paraded out and finally Valentine himself walked directly to the front of the Stage.

For a moment he acknowledged the forced and scattered applause from the crowd. It was no secret that Valentine was not the most popular lord of Festival.

He quickly intoned the ritual opening announcement.

'This - one - thing - that - I - was - going - to - wait - awhile - before - I - talked - about - it - but - maybe - we - should - talk - about - it - now - we - are - putting - the - music - up - here - for - free - we - are - bringing - the - food - in - but - the - one - major - thing - you - have - to - remember - that - the - man - there - next - to - you - is - your - brother - and - you - better - damn - well - remember - it - or - we - blow - the - whole - thing.'

Valentine paused and a senior textkeeper stepped forward, arms raised, first two fingers on each hand extended.

'The sign, people, the sign.'

Apathetically the crowd repeated the sign. Valentine

spoke again.

'My people, the giving has been good. Festival prospers and although some may say the spirit does not come to us, no one can deny we live well and with honour. The peace of Festival extends as far as man may travel...'

Valentine stopped as a voice floated clearly over the crowd:

'Horsepiss!'

A whole section of the crowd took up the cry.

'Horsepiss!'

'Horsepiss!'

The soldiers started to move forward as Valentine stood rooted, blood draining from his face. A beer jug shattered against the front of the Stage and a squad of troopers moved into the arena as more shouts came from the crowd.

'The outlaws are flying out of the west!'

'The outlaws – what about them?'

'Bring back Starkweather!'

'Starkweather!'

Suddenly Valentine's voice roared over the speakers.

'Shut up you swine! The Ceremony is over.'

He stalked from the Stage and the soldiers moved in to clear the sullen crowd from the arena.

X

Elly-May dug her nails into the burly skinner, faking ecstasy as he grunted and humped on top of her. Mentally she cursed herself for turning down a free ride into Festival for Celebration. The revelry there had left Afghan Promise half-empty and she was forced to make a token with tricks like this oaf.

Why couldn't she find more guys like the drifter who had got into the shootout with the troopers from Festival? He was a crystal freak and fargone too; turning a trick with him probably would have been weird and even painful, but at least he was pretty, and his eyes seemed to reflect more than the usual johns' that hung round Eggs's joint.

The skinner gasped and lay still. His dead weight forced her down on the hard bed. She wriggled to ease the bruises that still remained from the beating the soldiers had given her, trying to get information about the drifter.

'You finished, darlin'?'

The skinner grunted and rolled over. Elly-May got up from the bed, wiped herself and squeezed into her dress. She threw the skinner's shirt onto the bed.

'You better get dressed an' split darlin'; otherwise the boss'll wanna charge you for twice.'

The skinner raised his head.

'Stop hustlin' ya bitch, I'll go when I'm ready. Got it?'

'Don't tell me, darlin', tell the boss. He makes the rules.'

Despite his protests, the skinner began pulling on his clothes. When he was dressed he came over and tried to grab her. Elly-May ducked under his arm.

'All right lover boy, you had your fun. If you want any more you gotta pay, or I yell for the boys.'

Muttering, the man stumped out of the small room. Elly-

May sat down on the bed and began to re-draw the patterns on her breasts and eyelids with colour sticks from her pouch.

Fug this town, she thought, I don't know why I bother to get done up for most of these pigs. It wasn't as though she couldn't compete with the Festival girls: she had a good figure, breasts that needed no support, a slim waist, long legs. Her face was okay; maybe her nose was small and her mouth was a little too large, but the men seemed to like it that way; and her hair – she was really proud of its natural pure black and the way it hung almost to her waist, like in the text, 'rolls and flows all down her breast'.

Her thoughts were suddenly interrupted by a burst of gunfire on the strip. She jumped up and opened the window shutter a fraction. The strip was full of armed horsemen, firing into buildings and cutting down townsmen who ran frenziedly for safety. She slammed the shutter and pressed herself back against the wall. The unthinkable was happening.

Afghan Promise was being raided.

There was gunfire from the bar room and the wall shook. Elly-May looked around desperately. The only ways out were either through the window into the strip which was thronged with horsemen or through the door which led into the bar which, from the screams and shooting, seemed also to be a battlefield.

The door crashed open and a big shaven-headed man in a fur tunic stood framed in the doorway, holding a heavy shotgun.

Elly-May screamed and backed into the corner but instead of shooting her the outlaw laughed, lowered his gun and reached out and grabbed her by the arm. Elly-May struggled but his fingers tightened and he dragged her out into the bar.

Eggs and three of the boys lay on the floor looking very dead. In the corner three of the bar girls huddled, guarded by another outlaw. Elly-May was pushed into the corner and ordered to strip. She stood dumbly, unable to do anything. The outlaw repeated his order.

'Strip.'

'But I . . .'

The outlaw took a firm hand on the front of her dress and ripped downwards. The fabric rent down to her stomach and she reluctantly slipped her arms out of the torn garment, stepped out of her sandals and was pushed into the corner. The outlaw picked up her clothes and threw them into the street.

Two of the women in the corner with her were huddled together weeping. Slightly apart from them, her partner, red-haired Anna, sat against the wall looking resigned. Elly-May crouched beside her.

'Wha's gonna happen? They gonna kill us?'

Anna looked up.

'Maybe, maybe not if we come onto them. They're only johns, we oughta be able to impress them.'

'Why do they take our clothes? We gonna get raped for sure, oh Anna.'

'Listen, get yourself together. It's only rape if you struggle. Otherwise it's just another buncha tricks. Think like that an' maybe we'll stay alive longer. You hear?'

'Sure, but . . .'

'Okay, shut up an' see what happens.'

Two more women were brought in, stripped and pushed into the corner. Outside the gunfire became more sporadic.

Anna looked up and deliberately grinned at the guard.

'Hey mista, what you boys a-doin'?'

The outlaw looked surprised; most women they captured screamed and wept. He threw out his chest.

'We take town.'

'Plenty loot?'

'Sure, plenty loot.'

'An' women, you like women?'

'Sure.' The outlaw grinned.

'You get to pick your women?'

'Maybe.'

84

'Me an' me friend,' she indicated Elly-May, 'we can sure give a man a good time.'

'Good time?'

'Lovin' like you never had inna hills.'

The outlaw looked bewildered; southern women had strange ways.

'You not speak. I look for you in line. I remember.'

'You do that darlin'.'

Elly-May listened in wonder; how could Anna get into hustling in this situation? She seemed to have the right idea. Maybe they would survive.

Another group of women were dragged into the bar. The naked group in the corner grew steadily.

*　　*　　*

A sniper holed up on the roof of one of the few brick buildings was holding his own, preventing Iggy or any of his boys getting within thirty paces of the building. At the other end of the strip Oltha's foot men were herding a bunch of prisoners out of the general store. Two more houses were burning but except for the man on the roof and a group of maybe ten besieged in another building all resistance had ceased.

Celebration at Festival had left the town half-empty and it had fallen to their surprise attack with almost no trouble.

Soon the ammunition would run out in the pockets of resistance and it would all be over.

Cautiously Iggy moved out to where Winston was directing the fire into the house still held by the townsmen. He crouched beside the line of gunmen.

'Hey Winston.' Winston crawled over to him. 'Where's the chief?'

'Oltha? I think he's with his boys, roundin' up prisoners.'

'Lissen, let your boys keep the men in the house pinned down an' we'll get some of Oltha's bowmen t' let go a buncha fire arrows. Burn th' muthas out.'

Iggy and Winston crawled away. As they reached the

strip a cheer went up as a lucky shot toppled the man from his position on the roof. They hurried over to where Oltha stood.

'Hey Oltha, can you send up a buncha yer archers? We're gonna havta burn out those guys in th' cat house.'

Oltha nodded and made a signal. Five archers obediently trotted towards the building and Winston followed them. After a while smoke began to rise and the shooting stopped. Iggy turned to Oltha.

'Tha's it, the town's ours.'

'The fight was easy.'

'All down to plannin', chief. Now we gotta deal with the prisoners.'

'We kill.'

'No way. We need 'em.'

'For what?'

'First we need more men, an' some of the bozos in this town wouldn't be adverse to hirin' on wit' us. So tomorrow we give 'em the option. Ri'?'

The chief looked doubtful.

'Option?'

'Join us or get wasted.'

Oltha still looked doubtful but finally nodded.

'What of the old ones?'

'Let 'em go back to their homes. If we watch 'em they'll cause no trouble an' we'll need their skills.'

'I say kill.'

'Lissen, there's gonna be generator boys, blacksmiths, weavers; we gonna need that shit.'

'P'raps, although tribe manage without.'

'Yeah, I figure on some comforts.'

Oltha shrugged.

'So be it. What do we do with all these people?'

'Pick a big building an' herd 'em inside an' put guards all round. Make it clear that anyone who tries a breakout gets it. Ri'? Then tomorrow put 'em to work.'

'Work?'

'Sure, an' our own boys. The way I figure it, word's gonna

get back to Festival that we took the town an' an army's gonna come a-runnin', so I want the place sealed up tight; barricades, trenches, the whole bit.'

'Why not simply march on to Festival?'

'We gotta wait for more men. Lissen, you sent your messengers to the other tribes?'

'Yes.'

'An' d'yer think they're gonna come?'

'Hill raiders will come to burn Festival.'

'So how long they gonna be?'

'Four, maybe five days.'

'Then we wait a week before we do anything. Sit here snug behind our defences an' wait for more troops. If Valentine sends out soldiers we waste a bunch an' send 'em home.'

'You think soldiers come?'

'More'n likely, tha's why we spend tomorrow gettin' ready.'

Oltha thought for a while.

'My men will find it strange not to kill prisoners but your plan sounds good. I will give orders. What of the women?'

'Women?'

'We have gathered all the young women of the town in building.'

Oltha gestured at the now battered front of Eggs Akerly's bar.

'Soonly the tribe come, we Sing Dead. The men expect to dice for loot an' women. I get them to let prisoners live, but if no women . . .'

Oltha spread his hands; Iggy smiled.

'They'll get the women an' my boys too. Lissen, send a squad to bury the dead an' you an' me'll look over the chicks.'

* * *

More and more women were pushed into the bar and their clothes removed.

87

A side of the room was filled with forty or more women, every bar girl and hooker who had worked the strip, young wives, sisters and the elder daughters of merchants and craftsmen, and women who had just been passing through. A dozen lounging outlaws guarded them.

Suddenly the guards stiffened as two men walked through the door. Elly-May turned her head to see the new arrivals. The two men had brought no more women; they just sauntered across to the bar and helped themselves to drinks. She could see that one was a hill man, broad and, by the grey in his beard, probably in middle years, while the other... Elly-May caught her breath. It was him – the drifter. She grabbed Anna by the arm.

'It's him, it's him!'

Anna looked round.

'Who?'

'The one in the black hat an' cape, it's him, the drifter. You know, the pretty one who shot the soldier.'

'Are you sure?'

'Sure I'm sure.'

'Can you attract his attention? I'd like to get out of this meat market.'

Elly-May looked around carefully. From the manner of the other men, he and the older one had some kind of authority. Perhaps there was hope. Anna watched her.

'Are you gonna get somethin' together? I don't rate pulling no train for these hillbillies.'

Elly-May screwed up her courage, stood up and then pushed her way through the frightened women towards Iggy, but as she emerged from the group a guard stopped her and started to push her back.

'Wait, I wanna speak to him.'

The guard ignored her. Would she blow it if she yelled out? She didn't even know his name. Then he turned and saw her and the guard. He started to walk over.

'Whassama'?'

The guard stopped shoving her and turned to Iggy.

'Dunno chief, I . . .'

Quickly Elly-May interrupted.

'Please mister, remember me? At the table . . . the fight?'

Her voice trailed off. Iggy stared at her blankly for a while; then he grinned.

'I got started tellin' you about some trips, ri'? So? You want something?'

It was now or never. She took a deep breath, put one hand on her hip, licked her lips and, working as hard as she knew, said softly:

'I thought you might like to go on from where we got interrupted.'

Iggy burst out laughing.

'Far out, sister! But you maybe wouldn't dig all of it. You really think you're ready for anything.'

'Sure, I'd work pretty hard to not get turned out for the whole team.'

Iggy laughed again.

'Yeah, maybe you would. Okay, I got nothin' to lose.'

Iggy gestured to the guard.

'Let her through.'

Elly-May looked at Iggy.

'Listen, I got a friend back there, the one with the red hair, me partner, she's a heavy chick. The best in this town. I'd . . . could you get 'er outta the lineup?'

Iggy turned to a man who had walked in.

'Hey Winston, wanna meet the lady's friend?'

Winston smiled.

'Sho' nuff boss.'

'Okay babe, your friend comes too.'

'Thanks mister, you won't be disappointed.'

She beckoned to Anna who hurried through the crowd.

Iggy led them to where Oltha stood by the bar.

'Lissen, I'm cuttin' out these two, so you wanna take charge till dawn?'

'I post guards; we all party.'

'Okay fine.'

He turned to Winston and the women.

'You wanna get these ladies dressed up an' all. Then we find us the best house in town to party in. I'll cop the brews an' crystal.'

*   *   *

Elly-May looked at Iggy. Asleep at last despite the amounts of crystal he had hit up. With a lower tolerance she was still wide awake. She swivelled her head around the big room in the Shirrif's House. On cushions at the far side of the room Anna and Winston lay wrapped around each other. There was debris everywhere; even furniture was broken. It had been a heavy night.

After she had persuaded Iggy to take her and Anna out of the crowd of women, he had taken them to her room and watched them as they got ready.

She had done the best job on herself ever.

Having painted her breasts, mouth, eyelids, thighs and the flat of her stomach, she went to the cupboard and first of all pulled out her long boots. These were prized possessions, almost perfect pre-disaster relics that she had bought from a scavenger. Then she had brought out the long calfskin dress that was laced from her armpit to her hip and finally fell away to her ankles, leaving two slits that revealed her long legs. Anna had emerged in a wraparound skirt of local cloth and a beadwork halter that showed her painted breasts as she moved. If the two of them couldn't turn on these guys, she remembered thinking, no woman in town could.

And that was just what they had done. Since it was a matter of turning on Iggy and Winston in order to survive they had used every trick they knew and the two men had responded. Elly-May had thought she had known about male weirdness, but there had been times during the night when she had been unable to stop herself from screaming as Iggy giggled and revealed even more perverse tastes. A swap with Anna had given her the break which, at the time, she had felt was the salvation of her sanity.

Finally, though, Iggy had drifted off to sleep, leaving her bruised, aching and wide-awake behind crystal, but satisfied that her performance had been a success.

XI

Raucous laughter drifted across the walls of Festival and Joe Starkweather drummed restlessly as he smoked yet another pipe of weed. All evening he had tried to pin down Valentine to discuss the outlaw situation, but the lord of Festival had successfully managed to avoid him.

Finally Joe stood up and walked to the door. He looked tired and grim, if Valentine didn't choose to listen then he would have to be forced. By now he would be alone in his chamber with his current woman. He'd get mad but he'd be unable to run off.

Unquestioned by the guards, Starkweather limped through the corridors of the palace. He tried the door of the lord's chamber. Valentine hadn't bothered to bolt it.

A single candle was almost burned out and on the vast bed two figures lay wrapped in a fur rug. The floor was littered with black satin and red velvet in a crumpled heap together with white leather boots and belt.

For a while Starkweather stood silently; then he spoke.

'Valentine.'

The figures on the bed lay still.

'Valentine!'

Slowly the cocoon began to come apart and Valentine opened his eyes.

'Whassappenin'?'

Starkweather stood at the foot of the bed. Valentine sat up rubbing his eyes; then, becoming aware of the dark figure, he scrabbled for the pistol on the low bedside table.

'I wouldn't try shootin' me, Valentine; it'd probably cause a revolt.'

Valentine lowered the gun and stared poisonously at Starkweather.

'You better have a good reason for comin' here like this. I could call the guards.'

'I hardly think your guards are gonna try arrestin' me.'

An edge of panic crept into Valentine's voice.

'You're trying to get rid of me, aren't you? I heard them shouting for you today. You're plotting to become lord.'

Valentine raised the gun again.

'I've sussed you out. Honest Joe Starkweather, eighth lord of Festival, or will it be another stinkin' commune? I'll kill you first, Starkweather. You and the mob won't run me out of Festival.'

Starkweather's voice cut through Valentine's hysteria.

'Shut up an' put that gun down. I don't want your pathetic title.'

Almost as a reflex, Valentine lowered his gun again.

'Good, now keep quiet an' listen.'

'How dare you...'

'Valentine, shut up! I've come here to tell you that you're in more trouble than you can imagine.'

'All right, talk. I'll send the girl outside.'

Starkweather glanced at the girl.

'Let her stay. What I've got to say will be no secret.'

Valentine sank back into bed looking sullen.

'Do what you like.'

Starkweather's lips tightened.

'You're a fool, Valentine. This city is gonna be overrun by outlaws, while you screw obliviously.'

'What do you mean?'

'Are you aware that a caravan has been wiped out not three days away from here? That one third of the patrol you sent out has been killed by outlaws with rapid-fire guns only one day's ride from town? Do you wonder the mob yells horsepiss when you talk about the peace of Festival?'

'These are just rumours, you don't expect...'

Grimly Starkweather went on, ignoring the now frightened lord.

'They may be just rumours but rumours of outlaws mass-

93

ing in the hills, particularly if they're backed up by reports of a caravan raid an' a shootout, need to be checked out in some way. You can't just hope the trouble will go away.'

'I sent out a patrol didn't I? What else do you expect?'

'It's not just a patrol. The military are so untogether that Festival is an undefended city. Over the last few years we have relied solely on past reputation to scare off trouble. We can't live like that forever an' the people know it.'

'The people? What does that superstitious rabble know about Festival?'

'They are Festival, you fool, an' it's they who will defend it when necessary. It is your responsibility to organise that defence now, before it's too late.'

'Don't talk to me about responsibilities, Starkweather. A lord of Festival is responsible to no one but himself.'

'You are a fool, Valentine, your father was a fool before you...'

'You insolent mutha, you dare to insult the sacred memory of the sixth...'

'I knew your father, remember? He was more of a mincing libertine than you. He undermined the army, he let the merchants take over the administration of the city. Culture decayed, women were reduced to objects again. It was during his time that all the worst injustices of before the disaster were reintroduced to the city. His memory isn't sacred, in fact he's best forgotten. You maybe have one chance to undo some of his criminal stupidity.'

'I don't have to listen to this...'

'Oh yes you do, sonny boy, you have to listen, unless you want either the city to fall or your own people to drag you out an' hang you. If an invasion doesn't come, you can be sure revolution will.'

Valentine was white and silent; the hostile crowd at Celebration provided a solid reinforcement to Starkweather's words.

'What can we do? We could hire more mercenaries...'

'Mercenaries won't help you. Five hundred mercenaries could take over the city. The merchant retainers an' the guards must be put under a single command and an armed militia must be raised from the people . . .'

Valentine started.

'Arm the people! But you said they hate me, they might turn on me.'

Starkweather chuckled.

'Maybe that wouldn't be such a bad thing.'

He became serious again.

'You are gonna put out some sort of order, putting the city under some sort of popular control, a food-sharing system an' co-ordinated labour. If you don't, no defence can work.'

Valentine's paranoia flooded back.

'I knew it, you *are* trying to seize power.'

Before he could continue there was a loud knocking. Starkweather turned.

'Come in, it's open.'

Luther and another guard came in nervously.

'My lord . . . Joe. This man, he . . . rode in with news . . . he said . . .'

Valentine swung his feet onto the floor.

'Where is this man?'

'He's dead, my lord.'

'Dead?'

'Yes my lord; he rode in wounded, he died soon after. My lord, he brought news. I . . .'

Starkweather interrupted.

'Get yourself together, Luther, tell us what the man said.'

'Okay Joe, like . . . he told us that Afghan Promise had been attacked by outlaws. The town, Joe, it's fallen. Afghan Promise is in the hands of an outlaw army.'

The silence of shock distorted the room. Starkweather slowly turned to the half-naked lord sitting on the side of the bed, whose face was white with shock.

'I'm sorry for you, Valentine. I fear it's already too late.'

*   *   *

'Any fuggin' outlaw tryin' to break in here gonna get his.'

Wimp, standing shakily on a chair that seemed too fragile to support his ample figure, waved his shotgun as the crowd of revellers yelled and cheered.

'Ri' on, Wimp!'

'Ri' on!'

'You show dem fuggin' outlaws.'

Wimp raised his hand for silence and the shouting subsided a little.

'I tell you one thing, bruvvers an' sisters: we got to mobee-lise.'

Before he could go any further he lost his footing and toppled into the arms of the crowd.

Frankie Lee grinned.

The news of the fall of Afghan Promise had reached the revellers, the survivors of Celebration night, and they had received it with drunken enthusiasm. An army of outlaws was nothing to the fearless men of the Last Chance.

Wimp regained his position on the chair, amidst cheering, and carried on with his harangue as though nothing had happened.

'Mo-bee-lise, tha's what we gotta do. We gotta de-fend ourselfs.'

A man at the back of the crowd yelled:

'Fuggin' Valentine ain't gonna defend us, an' da's a fact.'

'Ri' on, bruvver, we gotta look out f'ourselfs.'

Wimp peered round drunkenly.

'We gonna need guns.'

'Ri'!'

'We gonna need ammunition.'

'Ri'!'

'We could turn this bar into a fuggin' fort.'

The crowd cheered, all except Harry Krishna who pushed to the front and demanded:

'How'm I gonna take care o' business if the place is set up like a fort?'

'If the fuggin' outlaws come, you ain't gonna have no business.'

'Yeah!'

Harry Krishna shrugged and retreated behind the bar. Wimp returned his attention to the crowd.

'Lissen, we want guns, ri'?'

'Ri'!'

'So who's got guns?'

About ten men waved their guns in the air.

'So we gonna need mo'.'

'Ri' on.'

'An' where we get 'em?'

Wimp paused and the crowd looked confused.

'I tell you! Off the fuggin' merchants.'

'Ri' on!'

The crowd cheered and a man yelled:

'What're we waitin' for?'

The cry was taken up.

'Yeah, what're we waitin' for?'

Wimp waved his shotgun in the general direction of the door and jumped from the chair. The crowd boiled out of the bar room and into the drag.

Frankie Lee followed on the outside of the crowd as they marched, still shouting, towards the Merchants' Quarter.

A large brazier gave out a red glow that illuminated the south entrance to the Quarter. The big double gates were shut and two retainers, one armed with a shotgun, the other with a pike, lounged against the wall. As the crowd from the Last Chance milled towards them they straightened up. The crowd halted, bunched up, about ten paces from the gate.

Wimp stepped forward.

'Open the gates, we wanna see Aaron the gunmaker.'

The retainer with the pike took a pace towards Wimp.

'You're drunk, go home before there's trouble.'

'Open the fuggin' gate, an' don't argue. Ain't you heard there's gonna be a war?'

Frankie Lee moved to the front of the crowd to see what was happening. The retainer was facing Wimp.

'I ain't gonna warn yous again, move on!'

He made a lunge at Wimp with the butt end of the pike but Wimp grabbed it and spun him round. The crowd roared with laughter but the retainer quickly recovered and swung at Wimp whose shotgun went flying as the pike butt caught him in the chest and he sat down heavily.

Wimp dived for his shotgun but as he brought it up the second retainer fired and Wimp sprawled sideways into the dust in front of the gun.

Then the pistol he had won from the rube was in Frankie Lee's hand and the retainer was lying in the dust beside Wimp. His partner dropped his pike and froze as the other men who had guns moved to the front of the crowd.

The crowd halted when a voice cut through the shouting.

'Disperse, or I'll order my men to open fire!'

Guns appeared through the embrasures at the top of the wooden stockade wall.

Nobody moved and both sides faced each other. Then heads turned as, to the crowd's right, the Arena Gate in the great Stage wall swung open and three horsemen galloped towards them.

Some of the men swung round and started to raise their weapons but then a cry went up. One of the riders was wearing the familiar leather coat.

'Hold it! It's Joe, it's Joe Starkweather!'

Starkweather pulled his horse to a stop in front of the crowd, beside the bodies of Wimp and the retainer.

'What the fug is goin' on here?'

Everyone began to shout at once. Joe raised his hands.

'Shut up, shut up! If you all start yellin' we ain't gonna get nowhere. Hey there, Frankie Lee, come over here.'

Frankie Lee holstered his gun and walked over. Starkweather sat on his horse and stared down at him; a lock of white hair fell over his eyes and he brushed it back with a weary gesture.

'Okay Frankie, how did this mess come about?'

'It was in the Chance, like. When we heaed about Afghan Promise the boys started to get worked up an' wanted to cop some guns. So we all came up here an' these creeps stopped us. Wimp was pretty fired up an' when this guy took a swing at him,' he indicated the retainer who was backed up against the gates, 'Wimp reached for his gun an' the other dude shot him. Tha's what happened.'

'Who shot the retainer?'

Frankie Lee studied the ground at his feet.

'Wimp had a lot of friends, Mistuh Starkweather.'

Joe studied the faces of the crowd.

'You better go on home, the merchants are gonna make trouble about this.'

Frankie Lee looked up.

'Beggin' your pardon, Mistuh Starkweather, but the merchants can go fug themselves. If the outlaws come them an' the lords are safe behind their walls. They got guns an' guards but out on the Drag we ain't got nothin'. Outlaws'll make mincemeat of us an' nothin' we can do. We gonna need guns.'

Starkweather regarded them grimly.

'You don't think the army'll protect you?'

A bar girl pushed to the front of the crowd and stood beside Frankie Lee.

'Lissen here, Mistuh Starkweather, us girls turn tricks for them solja boys ev'ry day. They treat us like dirt. If trouble comes they's gonna be up behind the walls defendin' the lords an' the merchants. Us folks on the Drag gonna be left to take our chances. We gotta have guns an' if'n we go home now we gonna come back an' no solja boys gonna stop us.'

A murmur of agreement ran through the crowd and another woman stepped forward.

'I came up from Afghan Promise for Festival; we was s'posed to be under the lord's protection there. Outlaws still got the town an' me ole man's most likely dead. Didn't get no protection there an' no reason why we should get any here.'

The crowd started to grow noisy again and Starkweather had to shout to make himself heard.

'Shut up an' listen! There's two men dead already. You

99

ain't gonna get guns by stormin' the gates. You'll just get yourselves killed. Go back to the Last Chance an' wait till morning. I'll guarantee you'll get the weapons you need.'

The crowd murmured but Frankie Lee and a few others began to walk back towards the Drag and the rest followed.

Joe Starkweather sighed and turned his horse towards the Arena Gate.

*   *   *

'... and under no circumstances will I arm the mob.'

Dawn light was filtering through the windows, and the audience room of the palace was filled with grim-faced men, representatives of the merchants, the guards, retainer captains. Valentine presided over the meeting from his carved throne. In the middle of the group Joe Starkweather stood facing him; his chin was covered in grey stubble and he looked exhausted.

'An' that's your final word?'

Valentine nodded. Starkweather shook his head and faced the merchants.

'An' how about you, are you gonna hide behind your walls an' pretend the rest of the world doesn't exist?'

The merchants shuffled uneasily, avoiding his eyes. None of them spoke. Joe swung round to where Luther stood among the guard captains.

'Luther, will you tell your lord exactly how long his precious army would last against a major force of outlaws? Are you afraid to let a little reality into this room?'

Luther looked guilty and uncomfortable.

'Joe, I...'

'Okay, okay. It seems you're all gonna follow that damn fool in his fancy throne, an' prop up his fantasy till the city's burned around you. There's nothing I can do here. I'm going out to the Drag to organise what defence I can.'

Starkweather took two paces towards the door but at a signal from Valentine the guards stopped him. The lord's voice cut coldly through the room.

'You aren't going anywhere, Starkweather. You're staying right here, under arrest until the emergency's over. Then we'll examine the question of treason.'

XII

As the sun dispersed the early morning mists around Afghan Promise the town started swarming with activity. Smoke of cooking fires rose into the clear air and the smell of food and wood smoke drifted through the streets. Gangs of prisoners dismantled buildings, constructed barricades and dug trenches under the watchful eye of armed guards.

Oltha moved through the camp, supervising the work and exchanging greetings with his men. He looked pleased as he paused to accept a jug of beer from one of the women. The work had started well; if it continued at the same rate the whole town would be ringed by a system of trenches and barricades by sunset. The highway would be blocked at each end of the town by a wall of rubble that left only two narrow entrances, just wide enough for a wagon to pass.

He returned the jug and continued his inspection, munching on an oatcake. He stopped to watch a gang of sweating prisoners breaking up one of the bars on the strip. More prisoners were loading debris onto an open wagon and Oltha walked over to the two guards sitting on the driver's bench.

'Greetings this new day.'

'Greetings chief.'

'No trouble from prisoners?'

'No trouble. They work, we watch. They know if they run we kill.'

Oltha nodded.

'Seen you Iggy this day?'

'No chief, we not seen him.'

Oltha walked on. Iggy would appear eventually.

* * *

Nath waited outside the Shirrif's House, hoping that Iggy would soon emerge. In a little while the door was pushed open and Iggy came out onto the porch, scratching his head and blinking at the light. Winston followed him out and Nath watched as they talked for a while; then Winston hurried off down the street, and Iggy yawned and sat down on the steps.

Nath walked over to Iggy, trying to make the meeting look like a matter of chance. He knew Oltha was suspicious of tribesmen who spent too much time around Iggy and his men.

As he approached, Iggy looked up.

'Hi, kid.'

'Greetings Iggy.'

'You look kinda nervous, whassamatta boy?'

'I wondered ... you have crystal?'

Iggy chuckled.

'Gettin' t' like crystal, are you?'

'I feel bad, lately. Crystal make me feel good.'

'Sure kid, make you feel alri', an' now you want some more, huh?'

'Yeah.'

'An' what if I don't have any?'

Nath said nothing but his eyes shifted dangerously. Iggy laughed.

'Okay, okay. You'll get your crystal, only remember one thing, ri'?'

'What?'

'You get this stuff off of me. Your fine ol' chief don' give you tasty treats like this. You jus' remember that fac', you hear?'

'I remember.'

'Okay.'

Iggy stood up and disappeared into the house. After a few moments he returned with a small box which he handed to Nath.

'There y' go, kid, an' don' forget what I said. Okay?'

*   *   *

After Iggy had left the building Elly-May stared out of the window for a while. Then Anna found a jug of wine and they shared it.

Eventually the discussion could not be put off any longer. It was Anna who voiced it.

'So whadda we do now?'

Elly-May shook her head.

'Dunno, we got outta the lineup but I ain't got a clue what happens now. Maybe we should just stay here.'

'Iggy's gonna get bored with us sooner or later. Unless he wastes us for fun first.'

'He's sure weird. I thought he was gonna kill me a coupla times last night.'

'He's a pervy little mutha, that's for sure.'

'He's pretty, though.'

'Shit Elly-May, you let any john with a face half kill you?'

'No, but it got you outta trouble, didn' it?'

'Sure, but I ain't too hot for many repeats of last night. Winston ain't too bad but one session with that Iggy nearly done me head in. I heard you screamin' an' all.'

Elly-May blushed and stared at the floor.

'Okay, so whadda we do?'

'I guess the first thing we do is take a walk outside.'

'An' get jumped by a team of horny tribesmen?'

'We can't stay here for ever.'

'I guess you're right.'

Across from the Shirrif's House some tribesmen were unloading sacks of grain from a wagon. They looked up as the two women came out of the house but otherwise took no notice. Elly-May relaxed slightly; maybe they would be regarded as Iggy's property and no one would interfere with them.

Her high-heeled boots kicked up tiny puffs of dust as the two of them walked slowly down the hot street, expecting to be stopped at any moment. As they passed more outlaws who looked at them without comment, Elly-May began to feel a lot safer.

At the end of the street a team of prisoners, stripped to

the waist in the hot sun, was building a barricade and it was obvious that the women could go no further in that particular direction. They turned into a side alley and started walking in the direction of the stream that ran along the back of the strip.

At the bank they halted and watched more prisoners up to their waists in water, driving long sharpened stakes into the stream bed. Further upstream women passed backwards and forwards with earthenware pitchers of water. As they came closer Elly-May realised that the women were divided into two distinct groups. Those carrying the water were naked except for strips of rag round their hips, while a second group, wearing homespun dresses and sandals, stood and watched clutching sticks and cudgels.

Elly-May recognised some of the women carrying water as girls from the strip. Bruises, weals and scratches on their bodies gave ample evidence of recent mistreatment. So that was what happened to the survivors of a night left to the disposal of the tribesmen.

She shuddered and clutched Anna's arm.

'Those are chicks from the strip!'

'Yeah, I know.'

'But look at the condition they're in. That coulda happened to us.'

'They're the lucky ones.'

'What happened to the rest?'

'I don' wanna think, I heard of girls tied across tables an' left for anyone t' use—an' worse.'

'Shit!'

Anna stopped talking as they came up to the line of women. She and Elly-May, in their provocative outfits, contrasted sharply with the rags and homespun dresses of the others.

One of the women struggling under a water pitcher stared hard from behind sweat-matted hair at Anna and Elly-May.

'Dirty slags, safe with yer fancy men while we were out there bein' torn up by those swine.'

Elly-May started; it was Lucille, a big, full-bodied girl from the Hyacinth House.

'Lucille, there was nothin'...'

'Don't talk to me you bitch.'

Lucille lunged at Elly-May but one of the tribeswomen swung her stick, knocking Lucille to the ground. Three of them gathered round and kicked her back into the water line. They shot Anna and Elly-May hostile glances but said nothing.

*   *   *

For a time Iggy busied himself moving around the town, checking the construction work and talking with his men. He noted the increased tension in his conversations with Oltha. The chief, he guessed, had a suspicion that Iggy was up to something with Nath and the other tribesmen whom he was turning on to crystal. It was possible to avoid Oltha for the most part, using Winston as a go-between. For a while he pondered the problem that sooner or later the chief would realise how Iggy was stringing out his men; then there would have to be a confrontation. He dismissed the thought from his mind; by the time the confrontation came a solution would present itself.

Iggy walked to the edge of the town and watched the construction of the barricades across the wide highway; then he strolled on a little way beyond the barricades to the start of open country. For a while he stared back at the growing defences. It was his town; he had come in from the hills; he was someone; he ruled his own town just like any lord. He turned, squinting against the sun reflected from the hot paving, and gazed down the highway in the direction of Festival.

One more week and his army would go down that road and then Festival would fall. The lands of the south would be his : the greatest territory that any man had held since the disaster. The years of running, of killings in the dark, of looting for a few meals and a bag of crystal were over for good. He was about to become a legend, far greater than Joe Starkweather or the Festival lords, greater even than Rooney the Crow or the half-mythical Ogoth. He would become the witch king of all the south, with power to rival even the fabled Djeggar.

His thoughts were cut short by the noise of the puller, across on the other side of the highway, dragging a felled tree towards the barricade. Its iron wheels rumbled on the pavings and high in the driver's cab he could make out the figure of Banana, stripped to the waist, hauling on the steering rods. He raised a hand to Iggy who returned his greeting.

Iggy slowly walked back towards the town, confident that with all he had going for him it would take more than Valentine and his half-assed soldier boys to stop him.

*   *   *

Elly-May and Anna hurried away from the women beside the stream. Since it was unlikely that they would be allowed past the barricades they headed back towards the strip.

As they turned into the strip, out of one of the number of alleys that ran back at right angles cutting through Afghan Promise's shack town, they almost walked into Iggy, standing talking with one of the tribesmen.

He looked up as they approached.

'Where do you think you two are goin'?'

They halted.

'Nowhere, Iggy.'

Elly-May looked nervously at Anna, but even her partner's solid confidence seemed to have drained away.

Iggy surveyed them coldly.

'Whaddaya mean, nowhere?'

'We jus' wen' walkin' tha's all, we didn' mean no harm by it.'

'Walkin'?'

'That's all, 'onest.'

'Got bored sittin' inna house, huh?'

Elly-May took a chance and smiled.

'Tha's ri'.'

Iggy leered.

'Too much energy maybe?'

Elly-May kept up the cheerful, sexy pose.

'You oughta know?'

Suddenly Iggy hardened again.

'What am I s'posed to know, babe? I don't wanna know nothin' 'bout you. All I know is that this is an army an' no rest home fer hookers, an' if you all so full of energy you better get somethin' to get behind doin', ri'?'

He swung round and yelled at two tribesmen who hurried over. Iggy pointed at the two women.

'Take these broads down your camp an' tell your women t' find 'em some work. Got it?'

The tribesmen nodded and Iggy walked off. One of them grasped Elly-May by the shoulder and pushed her down the street.

'Move!'

Numbly Elly-May and Anna walked in front of the two men, towards where Oltha's tribe had set up camp. Dimly they listened as the outlaws gave instructions to the head-woman. After they had gone the women gathered round grinning and jeering, their hands reaching out to grab Anna's and Elly-May's good clothes.

XIII

It was mid-morning and the Last Chance had rarely been so crowded at that time of day. It was not only the regular faces from the Drag, but labouring men and beggars from Shacktown and the North side. Although some were drinking and smoking pipes, the atmosphere was grim. For an hour people had been asking the same question: Where was Starkweather?

'I tell you, he's sold us out!'

A labouring man pounded his great calloused fist on the table.

'He conned you all into goin' quietly, he ain' gonna get us no guns.'

Frankie Lee turned on the man.

'Joe Starkweather's never let us down before; I don't reckon he's about t' start neither.'

The Last Chance regulars chorused agreement, but a beggar from Shacktown rounded on them.

'Yeah, if he's so much with us, how come he ain't here? You bar-flies got an answer for tha'?'

Frankie Lee said nothing; there was no denying that Starkweather hadn't kept his promise to show. Any excuse would only sound lame.

'Can't answer, huh? Mebbe yer precious Joe ain't so into th' people as he pretends.'

The Shacktown men began to mutter angrily.

Then the room fell silent as the swing doors banged and two soldiers in the lord's colours came into the bar and provided a focus for the rising hostility in the bar. One of Madame Lou's girls broke the tension slightly when, feet apart and hands on hips, she planted herself in front of the soldiers.

'Lookee, the brave solja boys 'ave come to protect us po' folks!'

The crowd guffawed but continued to edge forward, surrounding the two men in black surcoats. Harry Krishna pushed to the front, waving his arms.

'Hold it! Hold it! These boys are okay, it's Luther an' Mose, come in here alla time. Let's hear wha' they gotta say.'

The crowd fell silent and Luther scanned the still hostile faces.

'We ain't s'posed to rightly be here, but we split from the Gate detail to tell yous what happened. It's about Joe Starkweather.'

A murmur ran through the crowd.

'We heard you was waitin' for him to come here an' we came t' tell you, well, he ain't a-comin'.'

There were gasps and shouts of 'Tol' yer!' and 'Copout!' from the Shacktown men but Luther raised his hands and carried on.

'Lissen, yous got it wrong, it ain't Joe's fault he ain't here. The lord had him arrested. He's locked in the palace under guard.'

Confusion reigned as everyone tried to talk at once. The big Shacktowner yelled:

'Lissen, it's a con, Starkweather ain't been busted.'

The crowd shouted him down and, finding no support even from his partners, he then kept quiet. Luther started to look edgy.

'Lissen yous guys, me an' Mose gotta get on back to th' Gate, but we ain't kiddin'. The lord's got Starkweather locked up inna palace.'

They turned to leave but Frankie Lee stopped them.

'What the fug's Valentine busted Joe for? He's about the only guy who could save the city. He gotta be insane.'

Luther looked round grimly.

'Sure he's insane. Joe wanted to organise you folks t' fight the outlaws, an' it's the lord wen' apeshit at the idea of you folk bein' give guns an' had Joe busted. Tha's all I know, so we gotta split.'

The crowd parted and the soldiers hurried out of the door. Again everyone began to shout at once.

'Le's get 'im out!'

'Yeah, get 'im out!'

'Storm the fuggin' Gate!'

'Yeah!'

'Ri' on!'

Frankie Lee held up his hands.

'Listen, shut up. If we go chargin' up to th' Gate, more of us is gonna get killed, ri'? Jus' like Wimp. We gotta suss this out, 'cause I don't aim to go rushin' off an' gettin' meself wasted. Okay?'

'Okay? So what're we s'poseda do, bright boy?'

The girl from Madame Lou's who had confronted the soldiers turned on Frankie Lee.

'You got some master plan? Huh?'

'We're gonna need guns.'

Frankie Lee looked round.

'How many o' yous got guns here?'

About a dozen guns were produced.

'We gonna need a heap more t'get inside the walls.'

'Then th' only way t' get them guns is t' hit a gun-maker's, just them as is armed. Ri'?'

Frankie Lee thought for a moment.

'Hol' on, no dozen of us is gonna shoot their way into the Quarter. Tha's suicide.'

'I gotta nidea!'

The girl from Madame Lou's pushed to the front again.

'Back at Lou's there's ol' Ardbrass of the Chemical Guild sleepin' off a night wi' Dirty Rita. If we got 'im as an 'ostage we could walk ri' past th' guards, like.'

The big labourer pushed forward.

'She's ri', it's worth a try. Le's go get 'im.'

'Wait,' Frankie Lee raised his hand again, 'just a couple of us, ri'. A bunch of us raise too much ruckus.'

'So who's gonna go?'

Frankie Lee looked round.

'I'll go for one.'

'An' I'll go for anotha.'

The big labourer stepped forward. Frankie Lee looked at him.

'You gotta gun?'

'Sure.'

'Okay, le's go.'

*   *   *

The door opened and a guard came in with a tray of food. Joe Starkweather stood by the window. He could see, from its high position, clear over the walls and out across Festival to the woods on the south side, beyond the river. The day was still young and smoke curled up from a hundred breakfast cooking fires. Soon, he thought, it would be the smoke of Festival itself. When the guards had apologetically locked him in, he had first raged at the lord's wanton stupidity, but the anger had given place to a cold bitterness.

As the guard set the food down Joe turned his head.

'Any news?'

'No Joe. Only that Valentine is plannin' t' send a force to recapture Afghan Promise. Scouts have set out already to check it out.'

'Anything else happenin'?'

'Oh yeah, Luther said t' tell you that he'd tol' the folks on th' Drag 'bout how you was locked up.'

'Yeah, how they take it?'

'Dunno, don' think Luther hung round, he was s'poseda be on th' Gate.'

'Okay, thanks.'

'Okay Joe.'

The guard turned to go.

'Lissen Joe, I'm sorry we gotta keep you here like this...'

'That's okay. It ain't your fault.'

'Thanks Joe.'

The guard left and the key turned in the lock.

Joe Starkweather looked dully at the food.

*   *   *

Merchant Ardbrass awoke with a start as something hard and cold was jammed against the side of the bed.

'Shut up, or I'll blow yer head off, got it?'

Blinking, the figures of two men swam into focus. The one who had spoken was holding a pistol to the side of his head, while the other stood back a little and covered him with a shotgun. The one beside him glanced at the woman who lay by his side.

'Okay Rita, get outta bed an' keep quiet.'

Slowly and carefully the naked girl sat up, staring at Frankie Lee with wide, frightened eyes.

'Frankie, wha...'

'I said shut up an' get out!'

Frankie Lee's voice was cold. The girl slid out of bed, picked up her clothes and made for the door.

'Remember babe, keep your mouth shut.' Rita nodded silently and slipped out of the door. Frankie Lee turned his attention back to the merchant.

'Okay Mistuh Ardbrass, get up now, easy an' slow. Okay?'

Carefully, the fat little merchant struggled into a sitting position and, watched by the two armed men, swung his legs over the side of the bed. Frankie Lee glanced at his partner.

'Check his clothes for weapons.'

The big labourer rummaged through the merchant's discarded clothes and, having removed a small pistol and the man's pouch, dumped the garments on the bed. Frankie Lee stepped back.

'Okay, get dressed, but remember we're watchin' you.'

The merchant, aware that he looked absurd in his chubby nakedness, struggled into his clothes, sweating profusely. When he was finished, Frankie Lee backed to the door, opened it a little and peered outside.

'Everything looks okay, le's get goin'.'

He gestured with his gun.

'Start walkin' downstairs Mistuh Ardbrass, we're gonna be right behind you.'

The merchant looked round wide-eyed.

'What do you want with me? I don't have much money.'
'You'll find out soonly, jus' walk.'

The door opened out onto a gallery that overlooked the main room of Madame Lou's. Nothing appeared to have changed since they had come in. One-Legged Terry, who knew the score, was still sweeping up and everything was quiet. Cautiously they started down the wide stairs, guns trained on the merchant's back.

They paused on the porch of Madame Lou's and looked up and down the Drag. It was deserted except for two drunks and a beggar. Quickly they hurried the frightened merchant across to the Last Chance.

*   *   *

Valentine relaxed after the last of the court had filed out of the audience room. The morning had been exhausting but successful. He had finally rid himself of Starkweather and also bullied the merchants into providing two hundred horsemen for the expedition that would crush the outlaws at Afghan Promise. With another two hundred of his own guards the force would be more than adequate to deal with any rabble army of outlaws. Once that menace was out of the way, it would leave him free to stamp out the malcontents inside Festival itself and his troubles would be over.

He yawned and stretched his long legs. It was a nuisance that he had given orders for the army to move out so soon. He would really like to have resumed the sleep that had been interrupted so annoyingly by Starkweather.

The woman in the red cape had been really exceptional; it would probably be a good idea to take her with him when he rode with the army. Playing soldiers might be a novelty, but he would require other diversions while roughing it on the highway.

He took a pinch of crystal to ward off tiredness and reached for the bell on the small table beside the throne to ring for Lazarus. Moments later the old man appeared. Valentine stood up.

'Is my carriage prepared?'

'It will be ready soonly, my lord.'

'See it provisioned for two, and find the woman I had last night. Have her ready to travel, and then send the valet in to shave me and do my make-up.'

*　　　*　　　*

Inside the Last Chance the group of armed men gathered round Frankie Lee to receive their final instructions for the raid on the gunsmith's. Frankie Lee paused as the doors swung open and Claudette hurried into the bar room.

'Lissen fellas, I jus' heard somethin' tha's gonna make gettin' them guns one whole lot easier.'

'Yeah, what?'

'Well, I jus' met this solja boy who tol' me that they been ordered t' ride for Afghan Promise right away. Two hunerd from th' palace an' another two hunerd from the Quarter. It seems like if'n yous guys wait awhile you'll be able t' walk in with your hostage an' take what you want; only be a handful of retainers t' guard th' palace.'

Grinning, Frankie Lee turned to the frightened little merchant.

'You hear that, Mistuh Ardbrass; seems like our li'l plan's gonna work out fine.'

XIV

It was hot early afternoon and flies plagued Jaybee and
Slick as they crouched in the clump of thorn trees on the
hill overlooking Afghan Promise. They had been there
since early morning, riding close to the town under cover of
darkness, and then, as the sun had come up, settling in to
watch and estimate the strength of the outlaws. The morning had passed slowly but both men, experienced
scouts, dealt with the passage of time in their own way. Slick
with his bottle and his covert pipes, and Jaybee with the
almost inanimate stillness so characteristic of the tribesmen
of the far hills.

They were an unlikely pair: the fast foxy little city man
who had seen a hundred towns and a thousand bars, and the
slow solid hill man who rarely spoke and moved with the
maximum economy. Some chemistry had just seemed to
happen and they had been partners for many years, working together and hiring themselves out as a team to anyone
who would pay for their services.

This job for Valentine was, as far as they were concerned,
just another gig.

As usual it was Slick who eventually broke the silence.

'So how many you reckon they got in there? It's hard to
tell with so many comin' in all th' time. There's been tribesmen an' drifters ridin' in all mornin'.'

There was a long pause while the big hill man considered.

'Many ride in this day. I count ten times seven. Maybe
ten times ten times six already in the town. Maybe there
more; doubt if there less.'

'You hill boys got a helluva waya reckonin'.'

Slick paused for a moment to count up.

'So you reckon there's mebbe about seven hunred ri'
now?'

'Reckon.'

'An' about a third of 'em with horses?'

'Some ten times ten twice.'

'Two hunred horses an' five hunred foot: tha's what I figured an' they're streamin' in alla time. It don't look good f' Festival. I ain't seen an army like this gettin' together before. You recognise any of 'em?'

'Many tribes, many men without tribe. The totem of Oltha's tribe is raised but Oltha not plan this alone.'

'It's too big for Oltha to put together on his own, I keep seein' guys look like they could be Iggy's bunch. You reckon Iggy coulda dreamed up this deal? He's mad an' mean enough.'

Jaybee shrugged.

'Maybe Iggy. I can think of no other.'

They lapsed into silence again and scanned down into the town.

'Whoever's behind it they sure got the place sewn up tight. My token says Iggy's behind it.'

Again the hill man shrugged.

'We wait for dark and carry word to Festival? I see enough.'

Slick sucked on his pipe.

'Yeah, le's get back 'n' get paid off. I wouldn't take no bets on how long Festival's gonna last.'

*   *   *

Once the defences had been completed, there was little left to do around the fortified town apart from hauling firewood and checking in the new arrivals. The time passed with endless knife games, gambling and drinking. Occasionally a group of men would take one or two women prisoners to a secluded spot but even the rough sex play was becoming routine. Only the odd fight punctuated the waiting while the outlaw army grew to full strength.

For Nath the time dragged unusually slowly. Normally he would have welcomed a few days spent lazing around

117

in camp but his introduction to crystal had put a tense, waspish edge on his ordinarily solid personality. His paranoia was even more increased by the fact that he was out of crystal and it seemed that Iggy was deliberately avoiding him and leaving him to hurt.

He sat alone in the tent he shared with four more of Oltha's mounted guns. It was hot and stuffy and he brooded, turning over his dark thoughts and fighting the edge of crystal sickness that left him weak and sweating with a knotted stomach.

Suddenly through the tent flap he saw Iggy saunter past. Quickly he rose and hurried after him. Hearing footsteps behind him, Iggy turned.

'Hey there, Nath ol' buddy. You don' look too good.'

'Why you not come see me? No crystal, I hurt.'

Iggy stared coldly at the tribesman.

'You think I got nothin' to do but run round after dumb hillbillies who can't handle a li'l bit o' crystal? I got a fuggin' army to take care of, sonny boy.'

Nath's hand shook.

'I ... I hurting. You give crystal.'

'You got a whole bunch yesterday, ol' pal, so you jus' gonna hafta wait. So jus' fug off an' don' bother me.'

Nath's hand crept slowly towards his knife.

'You give crystal.'

Iggy stood quite still.

'Don't try nothin' boy or you won't get no crystal, never!'

He reached into his pouch and tossed Nath a small package.

'Here, but tha's gonna be the last if'n that chief of yours don' get off my back. He don' seem to like his boys doin' crystal.'

'Chief like mother hen!'

Nath spat and turned away to hurry back to his tent. Iggy watched him go, a grin stealing across his face. That should start something moving, he thought.

* * *

After three hits of crystal Nath began to feel more alive; the cramp left his stomach and the tension that had made him shake started to relax its grip. For a while he lay on the pile of furs that served him as a bed and watched the flies that buzzed in their ceaseless dance on the sickly air of the tent.

Soon, the crystal began to take hold and his thoughts started to flow as though on well oiled bearings. He sat up. Just one more hit and he would go out and check what was happening. Maybe find a woman or take his place in a round of the knife game.

He reached into his pouch, pulled out the package of crystal and unwrapped it. Just as he was raising the hit to his nose, the sound of the tent flap opening made him start, spilling the crystal down the front of his rawhide shirt.

'Curse on you, you . . .'

He stopped dead when he saw that the intruder was Oltha. Oltha stood in front of him scowling grimly.

'You take the crystal, you destroy yourself. There is no place for one who takes crystal in this tribe.'

Oltha's foot lashed out and the packet of crystal went flying, scattering its contents over the floor of the tent. Nath's surprise turned quickly to fury. He leaped to his feet.

'Tribe, tribe is nothing, you fool! I ride with Iggy. He deal with you!'

Oltha snarled and struck Nath across the face with the back of his hand.

'Out, pig! Leave this camp. I settle with Iggy!'

The force of the blow spun Nath round but he swung on Oltha and seized him by the throat.

'You wrong. I settle you! Now!'

Swiftly Oltha chopped him hard in the ribs. Nath lost his grip and doubled up in pain. Oltha stepped back and drew his knife.

'Crystal turns warriors into weaklings. Weakling must die!'

He raised his knife to finish Nath. There was a flash of light as a figure came through the tent flap. He turned to see Iggy standing just inside the tent, his face twisted into an evil smirk and a gun in his hand. Iggy shook his head.

'Too bad, chief. Too bad.'

Oltha took a step towards him, his knife raised. Then the gun exploded and, to Nath, it seemed as though a section of the back of Oltha's head just fell apart. His round spiked helmet rolled across the ground.

Nath gawped at Iggy in surprise.

'You kill chief.'

'Sho' kid, he was gettin' together t' waste you. I take care of my buddies, ain't I always tol' you that?'

Nath looked puzzled.

'But you kill chief. That could start war right in camp.'

Iggy shrugged.

'Maybe, unless . . .' He looked sideways at the tribesman. 'You tell everyone you done it.'

Nath became alarmed.

'Then tribe kill me.'

'Not if it was a fair fight. The way I heard it, if'n you kill the chief inna fair fight, you get t' be chief unless some cat challenges you, ri'?'

'Ri', but Oltha die by gun, and he only have knife.'

'Catch!' Iggy tossed his gun to Nath. He then pulled a second gun from inside his shirt and threw it on the floor beside Oltha's body.

'Now it looks like a fair fight, don' it?'

Slowly Nath nodded.

'It look, an' that makes Nath chief of tribe.'

'You reckon you can take care of any challengers?'

'None challenge Nath!'

*   *   *

At the sound of the shot, Slick took his pipe from his mouth and squinted towards the city.

'Those boys sure do argue some.'

He took another pull on his bottle and leaned back against the tree. Jaybee shaded his eyes to get a better view into the town.

'Crowd gathers before one tent. You got glass-for-long-seeing?'

Slick rummaged in his pack and produced a battered pair of binoculars.

'Here, you think somethin' cookin'?'

Jaybee peered through the binoculars for a while; then he lowered them and glanced at Slick.

'Shaman comes to tent. It means that a chief was in fight. Body brought from tent. Maybe chief, maybe Oltha.'

'If th' shaman's been called, somethin' up f' sure. Take another look an' see what's happenin'.'

*   *   *

'. . . And you bear witness that fight was fair?' The shaman looked hard at Iggy who smiled and spread his hands.

'Fairest I seen. Nath was jus' too good f' th' chief, despite the fac' tha' th' chief wen' for his gun firs'.'

'Then it is done.'

He turned to the crowd.

'All respect Nath as chief of tribe. If none challenge, then he sing for Oltha. Who challenges?'

Nath scanned the faces of the crowd. No one moved; then to his surprise he heard Iggy speak softly.

'If no one else'll challenge, then maybe I will.'

Nath opened his mouth but a vision of the wrath of the tribe if he revealed the deception made him keep quiet. The shaman faced Iggy, gripping his staff tightly with his wrinkled, tattooed hand.

'You are not of tribe. You have no right of challenge.'

'I figure I gotta right, by way of th' alliance I gotta right, an' by the fac' of we have fought in battle. Don't that give me a right?'

The shaman pondered for a while and turned to the crowd.

'Iggy claims right of challenge by alliance. Will any say him no?'

The crowd remained silent and the shaman again faced Iggy.

'How challenge you?'

'I challenge Nath to fight at sunset wi' hand guns under the common rules of gun law, as set down in th' texts of Cash.'

'That a rule of Festival.'

'Tha's how I'm makin' it.'

'Ways of Festival not ways of tribe.'

'Tha's my challenge. Take it or leave it.'

Again the shaman paused for thought. Then he raised his carved staff, the symbol of his authority.

'The challenge stands!'

Iggy looked at Nath.

'Till sundown, kid.'

Then he winked.

As the crowd carried Oltha's body away, Nath watched Iggy walk away and tugged his beard in bewilderment. Whatever Iggy was up to he could only wait and go along with it.

*   *   *

A fraction before sunset Winston pushed into Nath's tent. Nath, who sat loading his handgun, looked up watchfully.

'What want you?'

Winston studied the tribesman.

'I'm coat-holdin' f' Iggy, an' I jus' come over to see you got things clear.'

'I clear.'

Winston sat down opposite Nath.

'Le's jus' go over it, though, so's there's no mistake, ri'? You start from either end o' th' strip. You from th' east an' Iggy from th' west. Yous both walk towards each other until you think the moment's ri' an' you draw an' fire, okay? The one who draws first an' shoots straight kills th' other. Unerstand?'

'I said I clear.'

Winston stood up and made for the door of the tent. Before he stepped outside he looked back at Nath and winked.

'Iggy said t' tell you things ain't always what they seems.' Then he left.

A little later, as Nath walked to the eastern end of the strip, he couldn't shake the confusion that all the winks and the strange message had caused.

He took up his position at the end of the strip and suddenly realised that he had been manoeuvred into walking straight towards the setting sun. A hundred or more paces away, at the other end of the strip, he could see Iggy silhouetted against the glare. He was bareheaded, wearing only a shirt, trousers and boots. A heavy handgun hung in an ornamented holster. Nath stood still for a few moments, checked that his own gun rested easily in his belt and then, slowly and cautiously, began to walk down the strip. Squinting into the light he saw Iggy also start to move.

As they drew closer he heard Iggy call out to him.

'Hey kid.'

He halted and stood still, hand poised above the gun in his belt. Iggy kept on calmly walking.

'Hey kid, they gotta text in Festival that goes: "He not busy bein' born is busy dyin'," you believe that?'

Nath felt himself slipping deeper into confusion. His brain whirled; what game was Iggy playing? Iggy stopped, some ten paces away. His eyes had formed coloured patterns from staring into the sun. Iggy's long shadow reached almost to his feet.

'They also got an old, old sayin', kid: "Never give a sucker an even break".'

Iggy's right arm suddenly flashed into movement. Nath

clawed frantically for his own gun but Iggy fired and a crushing pain smashed into Nath's chest and he spun round and crumpled to the ground.

XV

A crowd, almost as large as the one for Celebration, gathered round the Highway Gate to watch Valentine lead his four hundred horsemen out to do battle with the out-laws. For the first time in many people's memory a lord of Festival was leading his troopers out of the city against an enemy.

The crowd milled over the highway and a line of guards on foot struggled to keep the approach to the gateway clear.

Further down the road Frankie Lee and his companions, guns hidden under their coats and the merchant Ardbrass bunched up in the middle of them, were waiting, mingling with the outside of the crowd that stretched out to the North Gate of the Merchants' Quarter.

Rank after rank of horsemen rode past, broadbrimmed hats shading their faces; guns bumping on the shoulders of their blue surcoats that carried the colours of the lord and the various merchant guilds. Fifty in all, eight abreast, they were the largest army to ride from Festival since Stark-weather had disbanded his troops. Alone in front of the column, Valentine rode a large black gelding. Although unpopular he still managed to overawe the crowd, sitting upright on the big horse. His black leather tunic with its gleaming metal plates, and his high black boots and black helmet with the circular gold design made him look every inch the supreme warlord; he had even received a ragged cheer from the press of spectators.

In the dust thrown up by the four hundred horses, the supply wagons and the carriages bearing the court ladies and textkeepers rattled out of the gates. When the last one had passed, the Highway Gate slammed shut and the crowd started to disperse.

Slowly, with their captive in the middle of them, Frankie Lee and his boys made their way towards the North Gate of the Merchants' Quarter. Although the gate was, as usual, open to the milling traffic, it was surrounded by extra guards who looked round watchfully. Obviously, after the incident of the previous night, the merchants were taking no chances. Frankie Lee signalled to the group to halt and turned to one of the men near him.

'Listen Ace, split back an' get your wagon, okay? Th' one wi' th' cover. We gotta be a bit suss about gettin' inside the Quarter.'

Ace hurried off and Frankie led the group back the way they had come and along the north side of the Backstage wall. As they rounded the corner of the wall and started to walk towards the arena, Ace came into sight, driving his covered cart drawn by a single mule. As he reached the little group of armed men he halted the mule and leaned over the side of the box.

'Wha' now, Frankie?'

Frankie Lee turned to the men.

'Yous all get inside an' keep your heads down.'

Then, as the men hurried round to the back of the wagon, he jabbed his gun into Ardbrass's ribs.

'Climb up onna box, Mistuh Ardbrass.'

The merchant scrambled up beside the driver and Frankie Lee followed, stepping past him and squatting down out of sight behind the wagon's cover. He looked round the men who crouched on the floor.

'Okay yous men, jus' keep it quiet till we're through the gate.'

He turned and poked Ardbrass with his pistol.

'Okay merchant, you jus' sit there an' act natural. Remember I'm behind you an' if you yell you're dead, got it?'

The merchant licked his lips and nodded. Frankie Lee crouched lower behind the box.

'Ri' Ace, take her away.'

The wagon bumped and rattled down the track that ran beside the wall, out onto the highway. Then it swung to the left down towards the North Gate of the Merchants' Quarter.

*   *   *

Joe Starkweather limped up and down his room. The enforced confinement was beginning to get on his nerves. From his window he had watched Valentine form up his troopers and ride out on the highway. He had watched them disappear down the highway with deep misgivings. If Valentine managed to lose a large portion of that force it would leave the city with little hope of defending itself in any way. He thought grimly of how it was quite likely that Valentine and his officer corps of posturing courtiers would lead their men into a total disaster. The fact that Valentine had rushed off with most of the troopers in the city, before the scouts had even returned to tell him about the size and organisation of the outlaws, did not improve Starkweather's opinion of the lord's military ability.

He ceased his pacing and futilely rattled the handle on the heavy wooden door.

'Hey guard, wha's happenin'?'

He hammered on the door with the end of his stick.

'Guard! Hey guard!'

For some minutes he continued to beat on the door and yell. Finally he heard a voice from the end of the corridor.

'Okay, okay, you ain't gotta beat th' place down.'

Keys rattled in the lock and a young, pimply trooper whom Starkweather didn't know stuck his head round the door.

'Wha's all the noise about, you lookin' f' trouble?'

'I'd suggest you use a few more manners talkin' to me, you punk.'

The guard stepped through the door, pulling a short club from where it hung on his belt. Suddenly recognition dawned and his jaw dropped. He lowered his club.

'Mistuh Starkweather, I didn't know it was you. I thought it was . . .'

127

Starkweather cut him short.

'Okay, leave it out. Wha's happenin' now Valentine's split? Are you in charge of the prisoners?'

'Me an' ol' Tom. There's only us recruits an' a coupla old 'uns lef'. Most everybody's rode out t' fight.'

'Pissed at bein' left to mind the fort?'

'Well...'

The guard looked young and awkward at this gesture of friendship.

'...Looks like it might be th' only battle in me time.'

Starkweather scowled.

'You think so?'

'Sure, after th' boys clean up them outlaws, I reckon it'll be a long time afore we get any more trouble.'

'You're an optimist, kid. Any word about what happens to me? When do I get outta here?'

'Captain never lef' no word, so I guess the orders t' keep you here gotta stand. Sorry, Mistuh Starkweather.'

The guard started to open the door but Starkweather stopped him.

'Anything in your orders that says I can't have a bottle or more weed?'

The guard looked blank.

'I guess not.'

'Okay. Then kid, you wanna run along an' get them for me. I got an account at the Chance.'

'Sure, Mistuh Starkweather.'

The guard slipped through the door. As the keys again rattled in the lock Starkweather sat down on his bed. The germ of an idea had started his brain working. Getting out might be hard but not impossible.

*   *   *

In front of the North Gate the bottleneck of travellers forced the cart to a halt. Beside them stood a group of hard-faced retainers who grimly surveyed the passing traffic. Frankie Lee pressed his gun gently into Ardbrass's back to

128

remind the merchant that he was still there.

One of the retainers glanced up at the wagon and spotted Ardbrass sitting on the box.

'G'day Mistuh Ardbrass.'

The merchant seemed paralysed. Beads of sweat were breaking out on his smooth chubby face. Frankie Lee pressed the gun harder into his back and hissed at him.

'Answer him.'

'G'day Oaks.'

The merchant's voice sounded strained and unnatural but the retainer appeared not to notice and the wagon jerked as Ace eased it through the gate. Once inside the Merchants' Quarter they were able to increase their pace; Frankie Lee watched as they bounced down the rutted avenue between the tents and banners of the various small merchants and the more permanent structures of the guilds and cartels. Finally they halted in front of a medium-sized tent. Above it a green banner fluttered, bearing the device of Aaron the gunsmith.

Frankie Lee climbed forward onto the driver's box and dropped to the ground. From the door of the tent old Johanna watched him approach with mild curiosity. She pushed grey hair back out of her eyes.

'Greetin's friend, wha' can we do f' you?'

Frankie Lee smiled and looked around at the tent and the banner.

'This Aaron th' gunmaker?'

'Tha's right.'

'I'm lookin' f' guns.'

'Pistol? Shotgun? We mos' likely able t' fix y' up.'

'I was hopin' y' might have a coupla rapid-fires.'

'Rapid-fires?'

Johanna looked dubiously at Frankie Lee's gambler's clothes.

'I better fetch me husband.'

'Sure, go ahead.'

A moment later Aaron stepped from the tent, wiping his hands on his oily apron.

'You lookin' for a rapid-fire?'

'Reckon so.'

Aaron inspected his fingers, then ran them through his thinning hair.

'You realise, Mistuh, them kinda guns don' come ... uh ... cheap?'

'I know, it's okay.'

Aaron looked straight at Frankie Lee.

'You better step inside.'

As he followed the gunsmith into the tent he gave a swift signal to Ace, then the tent flap dropped and he was inside the tent.

*　　　*　　　*

The keys rattling in the lock announced the return of the young guard. Starkweather sat on the bed and willed himself to keep calm. As the kid stepped through the door, clutching an earthenware bottle and a bag of weed, Joe stood up.

'Nice one kid, pass over the bottle an' I'll pour you a shot.'

'Gee thanks, Mistuh Starkweather.'

Starkweather splashed a liberal quantity of spirit into his mug and held it out to the boy but, as he reached out to take it, Starkweather's arm suddenly jerked upwards, throwing the raw spirit into the young guard's eyes. He howled and doubled up, desperately trying to rub away the burning spirit. Quickly Starkweather swung his stick and brought it down across the back of the boy's neck.

'Sorry, kid.'

The boy slumped unconscious to the floor and Starkweather jerked the gun and keys out of his belt; then turning limped to the door and out into the corridor.

*　　　*　　　*

'Sure is a nice piece.'

Frankie Lee worked the slide of the beautifully preserved pre-disaster submachine gun.

'You got any more?'

Aaron went to a chest and pulled out two more guns wrapped in oil-soaked cloth.

'I got two more but they ain't as good as that 'un. They work, though.'

'You got ammunition?'

'Thousand rounds for that size.'

Frankie looked impressed.

'Really? How many guns you keep here?'

Aaron thought for a moment.

'I guess mebbe twenty rifles – repeaters that is. 'Bout same of single shots – I make them meself, like. Then p'raps ten pistols an' a dozen or so shotguns.'

'No kiddin'.'

He paused for a moment.

'I guess I'll take the lot.'

Aaron laughed.

'You gotta joke. Valentine ain't even got that kinda trade goods.'

Frankie Lee spoke softly.

'Go outside an' look at my trades.'

Puzzled, Aaron walked to the tent flap and pulled it open. Facing him was Ace, the little merchant and the other men from the wagon. Except for Ardbrass they all had drawn guns. Ace pushed Aaron back into the tent and they all crowded inside. Johanna came in from the back of the tent but before she could scream Frankie Lee clapped a hand over her mouth.

'One sound an' y' husband gets it.'

Cautiously he released her. She remained silent, looking at the armed men almost resignedly. Frankie Lee glanced round the tent.

'Any more in y' family?'

'Two sons: Vernon an' Chet.'

'Where they?'

'Gone t' the wood sellers.'

'How soon they gonna come back?'

'Not for mebbe an hour.'

'You better not be lyin'.'

'It's true.'

'Okay.'

He turned and gestured to the men.

'Load this stuff on the wagon. Ace, you stay here an' help me watch these folks.'

Quickly the men from the Last Chance hefted the chests of guns and carried them out to the wagon.

When the last chest had been loaded, Frankie Lee motioned towards the entrance with his gun.

'Okay yous three, outside.'

'What're you gonna do with us?'

'Nothin' if'n yous behave. You're jus' gonna ride wi' us till we're safely outta the Quarter.'

Aaron, Ardbrass and Johanna squeezed onto the driver's box beside Ace, and Frankie Lee resumed his position just behind them. This time it wasn't the pistol he covered them with: in his lap he cradled the rapid-fire. Slowly the laden wagon bumped and rattled towards the South Gate of the Merchants' Quarter.

*   *   *

Joe Starkweather paused beside the door that opened into the inner courtyard of the palace. The exodus of four hundred soldiers had left the broad paved courtyard unnaturally quiet. A dog sniffed at a pile of garbage and women of the court strolled on the terraced top of the wall beside the Stage.

Beside the Arena Gate the door of the guard house opened in response to the clanging of the admission bell. A guard in a surcoat with the black palace colours hurried round to the big gate. Starkweather slipped back into the doorway and watched as the guard slid open the peephole and held an inaudible conversation with someone outside. The peephole was then shut, the trooper slid the bolts off the gate, swinging it open and a delivery cart from the Merchants' Quarter clattered into the courtyard. It halted beside the guard house and the guard hurried from the gate to help the merchant's men move a large barrel from the back of the cart. The gate stood open.

Starkweather stared at the open gate. The guard was occupied heaving the barrel into the guard house. It was probably his best opportunity to get free of Valentine's citadel. Taking a deep breath, he stepped out into the sunlight and limped hurriedly towards the open gate.

He had covered three quarters of the distance to the gate. The trooper and the delivery man had disappeared inside the guard house. It seemed that all was going perfectly. Then the guard stepped into the courtyard, saw him and raised his shotgun.

'Hold it right there, Joe!'

*   *   *

As Ace was about to urge the mule through the South Gate a retainer stepped into the centre of the track and waved them to a halt. Two more retainers stepped out of the shack beside the gate and joined the first, their guns held casually at the ready.

'G'day Mistuh Ardbrass, g'day Mistuh Aaron. We're sorry t' trouble you gen'lemen but we got orders to check all wagons headed for the Drag. Y'all mind steppin' down a moment?'

For a moment Ardbrass appeared to go rigid; his mouth was open like a stranded fish but no sound came. Then Frankie Lee pushed him to one side and, thrusting his heavy gun towards the retainers, crouched with one foot on the driver's box.

'Don' move boys, your orders jus' got changed. Drop your guns an' step back, an' don' get no fancy ideas 'bout takin' me 'cause with them scatter guns you'd waste these two fine merchants as well.'

Reluctantly the retainers let their guns drop to the ground and took a pace back, looking at the wagon uncomfortably. Frankie Lee turned to the men in the back.

'Okay, everyone out.'

The armed men scrambled from the back of the wagon and surrounded the three retainers. Frankie Lee jumped from the box and ordered the two merchants and the woman to climb down and join the retainers in the middle of the group of men. Then he looked round for the big labourer from Shacktown.

'You wanna go check out the guard post?'

'Sure.'

The big man ambled towards the shack and kicked the door open. Suddenly there was the roar of a shotgun; wood splinters flew as he was lifted off his feet and crashed into the dust, his face and chest hideous and bloody. Frankie Lee swung round and fired a long blast from the hip. The planks of the shack wall shattered under the impact of the heavy-calibre bullets. A figure appeared in the doorway clutching its stomach. For a moment it stood there and then pitched forward across the body of the labourer.

A commotion among the prisoners caused Frankie Lee to swing round again. The big labourer's partner had Ardbrass by the throat and was about to bury a long butcher's knife into the merchant's stomach. Frankie Lee jumped and grabbed the man's arm.

'Knock it off!'

In blind fury he lunged at Frankie Lee who, twisting sideways, dodged the knife thrust and clubbed the man across the back of his head with his gun butt. Then he straightened up and faced the rest of the men.

'If any more of yous got ideas of killin' the prisoners, f'get it! We gotta 'nuff troubles already.'

The men shuffled uneasily but said nothing. Frankie Lee gestured towards Ace.

'Start movin' that wagon out; th' rest of us'll stay here wi' the prisoners.'

Ace climbed into the driver's seat and prodded the

mule into motion. Frankie Lee walked over to the sullen group of prisoners.

'We gonna pull out now. It ain't gonna be much use you causin' any fuss 'cause you ain't gotta 'nuff troopers to take us even, but anyways we're gonna walk back to the Drag real slow, watchin' yous alla time an' you gonna stay quite still till we're outta sight. If'n you move you're dead. Clear?'

The prisoners nodded and, after picking up their guns, Frankie Lee slowly began backing through the gate; the rest of the men followed. As they retreated down the track to the Drag Aaron looked fearfully at Johanna.

'It looks as though we've lost everything.'

Johanna smiled, almost calmly.

'We still have our skills.'

XVI

Sprawled awkwardly across the rugs and cushions, Valentine slept fitfully as his coach bumped along the old highway on its solid wheels. The previous day at sunset they had stopped to camp for the night but the amounts of crystal Valentine had consumed kept him up past the dawn and it was only when the army was once more on the move that sleep had come to him.

On the other side of the coach the woman in the red velvet cape sat and watched him blankly.

Outside the coach the army rode in silence in small irregular groups that contrasted sharply with the neat formations of the day before. The sky was grey and overcast with a promise of rain, and a brisk wind whipped the cloaks of the officers.

The coach halted and the jerk threw Valentine into wakefulness. Blinking he peered at the woman.

'Wha's happened?'

'We've stopped, my lord.'

'I know that, you stupid bitch.'

He leaned out of the coach and shouted at a nearby trooper.

'Why have we stopped?'

The trooper reined in his horse and trotted to the side of the coach.

'The scouts're back, my lord.'

'Well don't stand there, stupid. Have them brought to me.'

'They're a-comin', my lord.'

Valentine opened the door of the coach and stepped down onto the road, stretching and easing his cramped limbs. Two officers rode up escorting Slick and Jaybee. The four of them dismounted. The two officers came to attention and saluted while the dusty, tired scouts slouched between them.

'The scouts are ready to make their reports, my lord.'

Valentine ignored the officer and studied Jaybee and Slick.

'So what have you men learned?'

Slick rubbed his stubbled chin and returned Valentine's stare.

'Well ... th' whole town's overrun by outlaws. Looks like a buncha tribes an' there's more a-comin' in alla time.'

'How many are there?'

'Well, we spotted Oltha's tribe f' sure, only I got an idea that maybe Oltha's dead an' Iggy's leadin' 'em an', o' course, there's Iggy's bunch an'...'

Impatiently Valentine cut the scout short.

'Just tell me how many; I'm not interested in the life history of lice-ridden outlaws.'

'Seems to me, could be useful t' know who you're fightin'.'

'Just tell me how many, damn you!'

Slick looked narrowly at the lord of Festival.

'I reckon maybe two hundred horse an' five hundred foot, only there could be a tidy few more by now.'

He glanced at Jaybee for confirmation; the hill man nodded. Valentine paused for a moment and walked round the two scouts as though inspecting them.

'You expect me to believe there's an army of seven hundred outlaws down the road?'

Slick turned to look at him.

'Near as we could figure.'

Valentine exploded.

'Rubbish! You're a liar, a fuggin' liar!'

The two scouts tensed and Slick, with a hint of menace, shifted his weight from one foot to the other.

'I'm just tellin' you what we seen. I ain't particular to bein' called a liar by any man, whoever he is.'

Valentine's face grew dark.

'I'm tellin' you, little man, there is no army of seven hundred outlaws. It is quite impossible.'

Slick shrugged.

'Have it your own way; I seen wha' I seen.'

*   *   *

Iggy stamped into the town flapping his arms to restore the circulation to his chilled limbs. He cursed the tribal custom that dictated that the new chief should spend the night on a freezing hillside honouring the spirit of the one he had killed. At least he had taken enough crystal to keep it up through the night and he was now the undisputed leader of the whole army. There was time enough to change the ways of the tribe once Festival had fallen.

In front of the Shirrif's House Winston met him with a bowl of hot soup. Iggy drank, cupping the warm bowl with both hands. He shivered.

'Godam rituals, I'm fuggin' froze.'

He handed the bowl back to Winston and looked around wiping his mouth.

'Anything happenin'?'

'Scout came in from down th' road. Seems Valentine's on the move with an army.'

Iggy's eyes flashed.

'No kiddin'?'

'Apparently there's maybe four hundred horse moved outta Festival yesterday an' were camped onna road. Scout figures they're movin' pretty slow an' ain't likely to get here much before sunset – oh yeah, an' Valentine's leadin' 'em himself.'

A grin crept over Iggy's face.

'Ri' on, fuggin' ri' on! We gotta start gettin' some sorta li'l party for these here visitors.'

*   *   *

The rain had started just after they had halted for the midday meal and then fallen steadily for the whole afternoon.

Luther, looking around at the soaking men and horses,

pulled his wet blanket more tightly round his shoulders in a futile attempt to ward off the damp. It was late afternoon and, by his reckoning, they should be nearing Afghan Promise.

Water dripped from the brim of his hat as he scanned the grey rain-blurred horizon for some indication of their position. It seemed as though they had been riding through the same featureless woodland for hours. Gradually something came into view that contrasted slightly with the uniform grey of the road ahead. As Luther drew closer he imagined that he could see a barrier across the road. An order came from the front and one by one the column halted. Luther kicked his horse and joined the group of men who stared into the rain. An officer peered into a telescope; after a while he snapped it shut and turned to the men.

'There seems to be a barricade of some kind across the road, but there's no sign of anyone manning it.'

The group looked at each other.

'What we gonna do about it, mistuh? Think we should carry on an' check it out?'

'Best stay here until the lord has a look at it.'

A clatter of hooves on the highway caused them to look round as Valentine and two officers rode up. Valentine reined his horse to a stop.

'What has the column stopped for? I gave no order.'

It was the officer who answered.

'There's some kinda barricade ahead, my lord. We thought it was best to halt until you had looked at it.'

Valentine gestured towards the telescope.

'Let me see what this barricade really is.'

He studied the road ahead for some moments.

'It does seem as though they have erected something across the road although I can see nobody guarding it. Here...' he passed the telescope to one of his aides, '...can you make out anything?'

The aide in turn peered down the road.

'It's certainly a barricade but I can't see anyone behind it.'

Valentine turned to the officer who had been leading the column.

'I think we should advance another hundred paces, then stop and look again.'

The officer bellowed the order to ride on and sluggishly the Festival army started to move again.

*   *   *

Iggy sat silently under the dripping branches of the trees beside the road, watching as Valentine and his men started to move again. Around him were fifty of his original boys, all quiet and tense, waiting on his signal to break from the woods and hit the column from Festival. Hit them and run for home had been Iggy's instructions and, as they watched, they realised that any kind of lengthy engagement with the far larger enemy force would be courting suicide although, after Iggy had distributed liberal amounts of crystal among his men, few bothered much about the odds.

When just under a third of the Festival army had passed the spot where they were hidden, Iggy raised his rifle and fired a single shot in the air. Howling, the outlaws crashed out of the trees and charged across the highway towards the troopers from Festival.

*   *   *

The outlaws cleaved into the middle of the column. At the sound of the sudden gunfire and shouting, the men at the front swung round and attempted to charge back the way they had come to aid their fellows; they soon became entangled with their own men from the centre who were attempting to get away from the attacking outlaws. By the time some order had been brought to the confusion, the outlaws had shot their way clear through the column of Festival men and were racing back towards the barricades, pumping bullet after bullet into the front half of the Festival army as they passed.

Valentine fought to control his plunging horse and screamed at the men around him:

'After them! After them!'

And with a number of his men following he took off in pursuit of the fleeing outlaws. Soon the entire army was heading for the barricade in a straggling charge. As it came near Valentine stopped and, turning in the saddle and waving his pistol, urged the men behind to greater speed.

Cynically he thought to himself that it didn't need him in the front rank to find out if the barricade was really unguarded.

*　　　*　　　*

As Luther and the rest of the men heading the charge raced closer to the defences blocking the road, he tensed for a hail of bullets from the other side, but then they were right on the line of overturned carts, furniture and heaped debris, and no shots had been fired. It really was undefended.

They bunched up as they hurtled through the gap in the barricade and then spread out again as they galloped off the highway and down the muddy approach to the town itself.

When Luther swung his horse into the main strip of Afghan Promise, the town appeared deserted apart from the last of the outlaw horsemen at the opposite end. Luther was surprised when, as the street filled with charging Festival troopers, one of the outlaws reined in his horse and looked backwards down the street.

*　　　*　　　*

Iggy sat on his horse and savoured the excitement of watching Valentine's men charging blindly towards him. Then, right on cue, his men hidden inside the buildings opened fire. Iggy laughed aloud as, caught in the savage crossfire, the Festival charge disintegrated into a milling chaos of shouting men and screaming, plunging horses. Iggy's horsemen returned and, in a line at the end of the street, added their contribution to the slaughter, ensuring that any Festival man who survived the terrible gauntlet of the men in the buildings would run head first into their guns.

*   *   *

One moment Luther had been charging full tilt down the main street of Afghan Promise and then, like some awful flood, the guns in the houses had opened up and the charge had turned in ghastly confusion. All around him men and horses had fallen screaming under the hail of bullets. His own horse had gone down and he was thrown into the mud. He had instinctively rolled away with his knees drawn up to avoid the thrashing hooves. For some time he lay on his side in the mud, stunned from the fall and the shock of the sudden attack.

As his senses returned Luther cautiously lifted his head. To his right a small group of his comrades who had managed to survive the murderous crossfire had bunched up and were attempting to break out back onto the highway. They had almost got to the end of the street when a heavy rapid-fire ripped into them and threw the leaders into a fallen tangle of men and horses. Those following collided with them and the last of the group were finished as they tried to get away on foot.

A bullet threw up a miniature fountain of mud close to his hand; desperately he rolled and scrambled for temporary cover between two dead horses. Further up the street he saw that a few of the others with the same idea were trying futilely to return the fire from the houses. Frantically Luther looked round for his own carbine and then saw with horror that it must have been lost in the mud when his horse went down. With a cold fear he realised that he was totally unarmed save for his knife.

Suddenly one of the men up the street broke from his cover and started running, crouched and zigzagging, towards where Luther lay. Almost impossibly he managed to evade the outlaws for about half the distance but then he screamed, twisted and pitched head first into the mud.

A realisation of imminent death gripped Luther. He knew that soon even the token resistance would be over and the outlaws would emerge from the buildings to finish those like himself who were hiding among the dead. Hopelessly, he looked round for something that might save him and like a miracle he saw a riderless horse galloping frantically down the street towards him.

He tensed himself; as the horse passed him he leaped. His hand touched a stirrup and he clung on as he was dragged bodily through the mud. His weight slowed the terrified animal slightly and halfway down the strip he was able to haul himself into the saddle. Bullets zipped by him with an evil buzz but none found its mark.

He was only paces from the end of the strip and the start of the approach to the highway when a figure sprang from the mud.

'Stop! Stop! For the prophet's sake, I beg you!'

Even under the coating of mud Luther recognised the black armour and pale face of Lord Valentine. Leaning down in the saddle he grasped the lord around the waist and hauled him up behind him; then they raced for the highway.

XVII

Joe Starkweather raised his arms and stood very still. The guard walked towards him, his gun pointing steadily at a spot somewhere in the centre of Starkweather's chest. Two paces in front of him, he halted. He was a thin cadaverous man with the dark, sunken eyes of a fanatic.

'Okay, left hand, pull that gun outta y' belt an' throw it over here.'

Carefully Joe obeyed and the pistol clattered on the paving. Without taking his eyes off Starkweather, the guard stooped, picked up the gun and stuffed it into his belt.

'Okay Mistuh Starkweather, le's jus' step into th' guard house.'

The guard shut the door behind them and motioned Starkweather towards a chair.

'Jus' sit down there, Starkweather, while I sorts out wha' to do wi' you. Escapin' ain't gonna make th' lord go any easier on you.'

Joe sat down and studied the guard.

'I don't know you, do I?'

'No, but I know you an' I heard th' way you talk to some o' the boys. Too many of your comnie scum in the guard if'n you asks me.'

'You a lord's man then?'

'Th' lord is by God appointed.'

Starkweather shot the man a penetrating look.

'You sound like a Christie.'

The man's eyes narrowed.

'I think you said enough.'

Joe suddenly grinned.

'I got it, you're the one they call Preach, ri'?'

'I tol' you to shut...'

He was cut short by the clanging of the admission bell. Automatically the guard jumped to his feet but then a look of confusion passed across his face. Starkweather laughed.

'Wonderin' what to do with me while you answer the bell?'

The guard pointed his gun at Joe.

'You're comin' wi' me. Try anythin' an' I'll blow your head off. I'd take pleasure in that.'

The bell kept up its insistent tolling as they walked out of the guard house.

Preach motioned to Starkweather to stand against the gate and without taking his eyes off him he slid open the peephole.

A shotgun barrel poked its black snout through the space.

'Open up f' th' people's militia!'

In one swift movement Preach, despite his surprise, slammed the shutter against the gun and threw himself back against the heavy gate. The only thing he was unable to do was to watch Starkweather at the same time and Joe took the opportunity.

His shoulder took Preach just under the ribs and the two of them rolled on the ground. Preach was the first on his feet and he aimed a kick at Starkweather who twisted to avoid it and grabbed the guard's foot, throwing him to the ground. Preach rolled over fumbling for the pistol in his belt. Starkweather's fingers came in contact with the barrel of the shotgun and, grasping it, he swung it in a wide arc. The butt struck Preach on the side of the head and he lay still. Gasping, Starkweather climbed to his feet. Keeping well out of range of the peephole he yelled to the people on the other side of the gate.

'This is Starkweather; who is that?'

A familiar voice yelled back.

'This is Frankie Lee, Mistuh Starkweather. We come from the Drag to get you out.'

Starkweather shot back the bolt and hauled the gate open. Outside stood fifty men and women from the Drag, armed and determined.

*　　　*　　　*

The meeting had gone on for hours and as Frankie Lee stood by the high window of the palace audience room the sky was growing dark and torches and watch fires were flickering into life all over Festival.

The crowded room housed representatives of all sections of Festival, many of whom had never before set foot inside the walls of Backstage. One faction was noticeably absent for, although Starkweather had himself tried persuading them to come, the merchants had solidly refused to have anything to do with the embryonic defence committee. Instead, they had closed their gates and turned the Merchants' Quarter into a fortified city within the city, denying anyone the use of their weapons and supplies. It was a serious blow to the defence of the rest of Festival: now they would have to make do with the few weapons left in the palace arsenal; the guns stolen from Aaron; and whatever personal weaponry could be found among the people.

It had not been too much trouble to organise the structure for defending the city. Starkweather had been unanimously elected to co-ordinate the entire operation, basing himself in the palace. The rest of the city would be split into three sections. The Northside would take care of both their own defence and any attack from along the highway; they would be under the command of Mac the Smith and Nasty Elaine. The Shacktowners under the Radio Kid would watch the south and east, dividing the southern boundary (marked by the river) with the boys from the Drag under Frankie Lee who would also take care of the west side up to the Merchants' Quarter. Old Tom and the remaining guards would look after the defence of Backstage itself; all except Preach and four others who opted to remain loyal to Valentine and had been confined under guard. The fortification of the city was to start at dawn.

Only one question had remained unanswered: what would happen when Valentine returned? The Shacktowners and the Drag crew wanted the lord arrested and the city declared a commune, while the more conservative Northside and palace staff merely wanted the lord's power limited by a council of representatives.

Starkweather listened in silence as the argument went round and round. Finally, after the debate threatened to run into its third hour, he held up his hand for silence.

'It seems to me that we're all gettin' heated up 'bout somethin' that may not happen. If Valentine handles this campaign like he handles mos' everythin' else I doubt if he'll be returnin' at all. If by some miracle he does put down the outlaws, then we got nothin' to worry about. I think we sh'd carry on with the defence an' sort out the problems of lords an' such after the danger has passed.'

The Radio Kid, one of the strongest in favour of the lord's arrest, stood up.

'Lissen Joe, s'pose Valentine comes back an' he's lost his army an' the outlaws are on his tail – wha' we gonna do then? You gotta admit it's quite likely.'

'If that happens then we confine him till after the outlaws have been dealt with an' then sort it out. Okay?'

There were murmurs of agreement and the meeting began to break up.

When everyone had left Starkweather sat for a while in thought. He looked up and saw a figure, dimly visible in the candlelight, standing at the other end of the room.

'Who is that?'

Starkweather squinted into the gloom, atempting to distinguish features. The figure came forward.

'It's me, Mistuh Starkweather – Wheatstraw the text-keeper. I was wonderin' if I could be useful to you.'

Starkweather laughed.

'I thought it was common knowledge that I set no great store by your texts.'

Wheatstraw looked at him intently.

'In time of trouble men will accept counsel from many unsual quarters.'

'And would you counsel me, brother textkeeper?'

'The counsel of the texts has been with us from the start.'

'You've become as obscure as your damned prophet. What text have you that relates to our current dilemma?'

The textkeeper smiled.

'I have searched the subject; only the obvious – "Do what you think you should do".'

'Too easy, brother, too easy. Come again when you can be specific. Even I know the next lines.'

*   *   *

The morning dawned grey and overcast and a brisk wind from the east hinted at coming rain. Frankie Lee's cape billowed around him as he stood outside the Last Chance and watched the team of men boarding up the windows and stacking the front porch with bags of earth. Further down another team was dismantling the flat figure of a stripper, three times normal size, that was the main feature of the facia of Cindy's Pleasure Parlour.

He turned and hurried across the Drag to Madame Lou's where a file of men and women came and went, checking in their personal weapons for the common defence and drawing assignments in case of attack. As he crossed the street he glanced down its length at the squad digging trenches where the Drag joined the Arena.

More men swarmed over the front of Madame Lou's, building the same kind of fortifications that were going up at the Last Chance. Further back down the street one of the smaller bars was being dismantled to provide materials.

Inside Madame Lou's there was another scene of frenzied activity. A long table had been set up in the centre of the main parlour; at one end of it Lou herself, bracelets jingling, checked the guns that were brought in, recording the owner's name in a ledger and passing them to One-Legged Terry to be stacked against the wall. At the other end of the table Harry Krishna was dealing with volunteers and assigning them to the various squads. Frankie Lee stood behind Madame Lou until she had dealt with the line of people bringing in weapons. When the last one had moved onto Harry Krishna, he leaned over and spoke to her.

'How's it goin' – how're we doin' for guns?'

Madame Lou looked up and brushed a stray wisp of blonde hair out of her eyes.

'It ain't goin' too bad, Frankie.'

She ran her finger down the list.

'We got thirty brung in since midnight an' they keep a-comin'.'

She paused as a gambler came in and placed a pair of pistols on the table.

'I come t' sign on for th' defence. 'M I gonna get these pieces back when it's all over?'

'Sure, I check y' name in th' book an' if'n y' don' get wasted y' get y' guns back, okay?'

'Okay.'

Madame Lou scribbled the man's name in her book, directed him to Harry Krishna and turned back to Frankie Lee.

'Problem we gonna have is ammunition. I mean, like, we got thirty pieces, ri', but not more'n two hunred rounds have come in altogether an' I don' see more a-comin' in, 'cept in the same amounts, say six or seven wi' each gun.'

'Tha's a problem. We got maybe three thousand rounds wi' the guns we nicked off Aaron but tha's gonna be spread roun' the whole city. I don' see us endin' up with more'n fifty guns an' maybe twenty rounds for each gun.'

Madame Lou shook her head.

'It's the best we can do. There's plenty bows an' the girls're bustin' a gut makin' arrows.'

'Wha' 'bout horses?'

'They're all goin' behin' the walls so Joe's got some cavalry to play wi'.'

Frankie Lee nodded.

'Many people pullin' out?'

Madame Lou shook her head.

'Not from aroun' here; only a few o' the fast boys who split to join the outlaws. But I heard a lotta the Northside families had moved out, a-headin' out through the swamps.'

'An' are many boys signin' up to fight?'

'Enough.'

'Good. Lissen, I'm gonna take a walk an' see how they're doin' puttin' stakes across the river, okay?'

'Okay, see you later.'

Frankie Lee walked out the door, pausing to make room for a man who came in carrying an ancient shotgun to add to the arsenal.

*   *   *

Through the morning the PA regularly crackled into life as announcements and information were broadcast across Festival. Most normal business had ceased and a constant stream of outlying homesteaders poured in to take refuge in the city. With the Merchants' Quarter sealed off, food was becoming a problem and, in addition to the regular pleas for arms and volunteers, Isaac Feinberg started putting out requests that private stocks of food be turned over to the defence committee for rationed distribution.

Joe Starkweather seemed to be everywhere: checking, urging, discussing problems with the squads of men putting in the defences. Festival seemed like a transformed city as he rode through it. The normal apathy and corruption seemed to have been stripped away in the face of the threat of attack. Even the rain that began to fall soon after noon and quickly transformed the streets of the city into seas of mud could not slow down the work. Deep in the back of Starkweather's mind, beneath the cursing and enthusiasm, the thought lurked that in all probability the effort had come too late.

XVIII

As Luther and Valentine raced out of Afghan Promise, the men that Iggy had positioned on the barricades to cut off any Festival men who managed to escape the shambles on the main street were already picking through the fallen, shooting the wounded and collecting the weapons of the dead. For them the battle was over and the appearance of the two men on the single horse took them completely by surprise. A few shots were loosed at them as they galloped through the gap in the barricades but after that they quickly rode into freedom beyond the range of the outlaws' guns.

Once they were safely down the highway, Luther reined in the foaming horse and stopped. He looked grimly back at Valentine.

'Best we dismount an' walk the horse f' a while. If we run it any more wi' two of us up it'll cave in.'

White and shaking Valentine dismounted.

'What happens if they come after us?'

'I don' think they'll be a-huntin' for us yet a while an' a dead horse ain't gonna be no use at all. Like I said, best we walk a while.'

Valentine stared hard at Luther.

'Are you tryin' to give me orders?'

Luther faced Valentine grimly.

'Take it how you like. I don' think you're in any space t' tell anyone wha' to do.'

'Damn your insolence...'

'Shut th' fug up! You led us into that death trap back there an' I for one ain't takin' no more bullshit. So you do what I say or I'll jus' ride off an' leave you. Got it?'

Valentine clenched his fist and grew two shades paler but as the trooper began to walk off leading the horse he fell into step behind him.

For a while they walked in silence until the sound of hooves on the road in front of them made Luther halt and listen. Then, grabbing Valentine by the arm and dragging the horse behind him, he ran for the trees.

*   *   *

Carefully Iggy wiped the rain from his gun as he stood in the shelter of the porch of the Shirrif's House and watched Winston and his men salvaging weapons from the dead who lay in the mud of the main street.

'Hey Winston, come over here. Let them hill boys root through th' mud for guns. I wanna talk to you.'

Winston hurried over to where Iggy stood grinning.

'You want me?'

Iggy paused for a moment staring over the scene of desolation.

'I guess Festival's gotta be ours for th' takin', huh?'

Winston looked back over the bloody swamp that was the Afghan Promise strip.

'Mus' be the end of their army.'

'Fuggin' sho' it is. Like shootin' fish in a barrel, hey? You enjoy the fight?'

A slightly troubled look crossed Winston's face.

'A lotta good men wen' down. We never wasted so many before.'

Iggy's grin faded and his eyes became hard.

'You goin' soft on me?'

'No, it's jus'...'

'Jus' what?'

'I dunno, it jus' seemed too easy. I like t' see a fight, not jus' sit tight an' butcher the opposition.'

'You still pissed off 'cause I didn' let you ride out wi' the decoy party?'

Winston hesitated.

'Maybe, I dunno. F'get it.'

Iggy eyed him carefully.

'There's gonna be plenty of fightin' f' you to get into.'

152

'Yeah sho'. I'm okay; jus' was a lotta killin', takes gettin' used to.'

'Sho'.'

For a while the two men stood in silence looking at the street. Bodies of men and horses formed grotesque humps so mud-covered that they were indistinguishable from the street itself except by their twisted shapes. After a while Iggy turned towards the door. As he opened it he glanced at Winston.

'You send out the detail to pick up their supply wagons?'

'Sho', they wen' off even before we stopped shootin'.'

'Good, le's go have us a drink.'

*   *   *

Valentine and Luther crouched in the wet bushes as a group of outlaws rode by escorting the Festival supply wagons. Silently they watched as the outlaws passed laughing and joking. The horse became restless and Luther straightened to stroke its head and quieten it. The outlaws appeared not to notice and rode on, passing around bottles of spirit obviously looted from the wagons. In front of one of the outlaws sat the girl in the red cape, her head sunk on her chest and hands tied in front of her. Valentine's knuckles whitened but he remained still.

For some time after the outlaws had passed they remained hidden in the trees. Then Luther led the horse out onto the road, mounted and helped Valentine to climb up behind him.

They rode at an easy pace through the steadily falling rain for what seemed like hours. Cold seeped through their bodies and both men's teeth began to chatter; it was only when the cold and damp started to become intolerable that Valentine broke the silence.

'How long will it take to get to Festival?'

Luther looked round. Lost in his own thoughts he had almost forgotten the lord behind him.

'If we rode through the night I guess we could be there by dawn.'

Valentine shivered.

'We'll die of chills before the dawn.'

Luther pulled his foot out of the stirrup and flexed his cramped muscles.

'You could be right at that. We oughta stop although we'll make no fire in this rain. Best go on as long as we can.'

Again they rode on silently and the clouded sky began to grow dark. Luther now knew that Valentine had been right. He was shivering constantly and was certain that the chills would get through to them before they ever reached Festival. Their problems were increased by the fact that they had emerged from the woodland and were riding across open hillside at the full mercy of the wind and rain. Then, as the hill fell away to their left into a long valley, he saw something through the rain. It seemed like a cluster of buildings halfway down the valley, either a homestead or, more likely, a ruined farm: there were no lights showing and no sign of life.

He turned to look back at Valentine.

'There seems to be some kinda buildin' down there. I think we oughta take a look.'

'Anything that will give us shelter.'

Luther guided the horse through a gap in the rotting fence beside the highway and set off down the hillside. At the bottom they came onto a rough track that led from the distant building to join the highway at a point further on.

As they drew closer to the buildings Luther was able to see, through the dust, that it was in fact an oldtime farm, although it seemed in good repair and some of the outbuildings were of recent construction. At the end of the track an opened gate revealed a paved yard. Drawing level with it Luther halted and signalled to Valentine to dismount, then swung to the ground himself and handed the reins to the lord.

154

'You got any kinda weapon?'

Valentine reached under his cloak and produced a pistol.

'I'm afraid it's empty.'

Luther cursed but took the gun.

'Wait here while I look round.'

Walking cautiously on the balls of his feet to stop his boot heels ringing on the paved yard, Luther crept towards the farmhouse. Nothing moved. He got to the wall, stopped and looked around: still no sign of life. Gently he eased himself along the wall until he reached the doorway. Reaching carefully for the handle, he turned it and pushed. The door creaked open; no sound or movement came from within. In one action he swung round and sprang inside the house, immediately sidestepping so that he would not be silhouetted against the open door.

Crouching inside he stared round the dark room. It seemed empty and he fumbled in his pouch for a lighter. Three times he struck the flint on the steel but the wick refused to catch fire. He cursed under his breath: maybe the godam thing had got wet. On the fourth try it flared into life.

The flickering light revealed a deserted room, tidy, furnished, but devoid of people. An oil lamp stood on the table in the middle and Luther lit it. It was a pleasant farmhouse kitchen. A big dresser stood against one wall holding rows of pots and crockery. Cured hams hung from the ceiling beams and a black iron stove filled the chimney-piece. There was even a barrel of ale standing in one corner. Obviously a family of farmers had lived there until very recently but now they had gone; maybe they had fled to the east, away from the menace of the outlaws.

After a final look round Luther turned back to the door and yelled to Valentine.

'Okay, it's empty. C'mon in.'

Valentine came towards him leading the horse.

'Will you do something about this animal?'

Luther pointed across the yard.

'Put it in the stable, there may even be feed for it.'

Valentine compressed his lips but said nothing and tugged the horse in the direction of the barn.

*   *   *

Luther relaxed himself into the soft bed. The farmhouse had provided everything they had needed: a meal of cold ham and pickles, a fire to warm them and dry their wet clothes, beer and even a proper bed. The lord had eaten quickly and in silence and then retired to bed. For some time Luther sat in front of the stove, quietly going over the massacre at Afghan Promise and the progressive stages of stupidity that had led them into it. Eventually weariness had overcome him and he too had searched for a bed.

For a long while he hovered on the brink of sleep, alternating between drifting out and being brought back to consciousness by recurring images of the day's events.

A noise in the yard brought him fully awake. He held his breath and listened. He could clearly distinguish the sound of heavy boots on the pavings and of whispered conversation.

Silently he slid out of bed, wrapping a blanket round himself. Maybe it was the farm people returning or maybe outlaw scouts. He picked up the empty pistol from beside the bed and padded barefoot to the top of the stairs. For a moment he hesitated and carefully, one step at a time, crept down them. At the halfway bend he froze as the door to the yard swung open and moonlight streamed into the kitchen. Two dark figures crept cautiously through the door. Luther watched and waited. A light flared, illuminating a mud-spattered surcoat still clearly bearing the colours of the Chemical Guild. Luther stepped forward, coming down into the room. At the sudden movement one of the men raised his gun. Luther halted.

'Take it easy! It's me, Luther from the palace guard.'

The gun wavered.

'Wha' the fug are you doin' here?'

Luther came forward again.

'Jus' crashin' f' the night. Light th' lamp on th' table an' we'll be able to see each other.'

The lamp glowed into life revealing two men in Guild colours. The second man spoke quickly to the one with the gun:

'It is! Tha's Luther, I seen him before.'

He peered at Luther.

'You escape that blood bath too?'

Luther sat down.

'I don' wanna go over it again.'

He paused.

'Lissen, you might as well make y'selfs at home. There's food an' beer an' even beds. Wha' you done wi' your horses?'

'We ain't got no horses; they're lyin' in the mud at that godam town.'

'You walked here?'

'Tha's ri'.'

'Shit.'

There was silence as the two men investigated the food and beer. As they ate, the one with the gun glanced at Luther.

'Anyone else get away wi' you?'

'Sure, Lord Valentine's asleep upstairs.'

The man jumped to his feet and picked up his shotgun.

'That son of a bitch asleep wi' all them good men dead on his account. He ain't gonna sleep f' long.'

Luther stood up.

'Hold it, hold it! He's gonna be more use to us alive in Festival than layin' dead here.'

Reluctantly the man sat down.

'Maybe you're right, but I sure hate to see that mutha walkin' round livin'.'

*　　*　　*

Valentine awoke just as the eastern sky was starting to

grow light. Before falling asleep he had planned what he was going to do.

He stealthily crawled out of bed and made his way to the stairs and down to the kitchen.

Locating his clothes, now almost dry, he quickly dressed, then eased open the outside door and hurried across the yard in the direction of the stables.

In a matter of minutes he had saddled the horse and was mounted and heading along the track towards the highway.

*　·　*　　　*

The sun was high as he approached Festival and the rain-soaked landscape was slowly drying out. As he galloped down the final stretch of highway he saw that a barricade had been erected across the road in an almost identical manner to the one built by the outlaws at Afghan Promise.

For a moment he panicked and started to turn his horse. Could it be that they were already there? Then he realised that it was simply not possible for the outlaws to have marched and taken the city in so short a space of time. The barrier had probably been erected by the merchants as a defence measure.

As he came up to the barricade a labourer appeared pointing a crossbow at him.

'Halt or I fire.'

Valentine pulled his horse to a stop.

'Put down that ridiculous weapon, you fool. Don't you recognise the lord of the city?'

The man disappeared and a portion of the barricade was pulled to one side. Valentine urged his horse forward.

Suddenly he was surrounded by a crowd of ragged labourers, all holding weapons and all levelling them at him. One of them seized his horse's bridle and looked up at him.

'You'd better dismount, Valentine. I'm arrestin' you in the name of the People's Defence Committee.'

XIX

The town hummed with activity as the outlaw army prepared to move out. Elly-May found herself, along with the other slave women, running backwards and forwards carrying bundles of provisions from the tents to the supply wagons.

Life in the outlaw camp was still hard and sordid for the captured women but not like the hell of the first day when Iggy had handed her and Anna over to the tribeswomen who had stripped and beaten them, then divided their clothes and thrown them ragged loin cloths to cover their nakedness. After that, the open brutality both from the outlaw women and from the other captives that seemed rooted in their jealousy of the initial attention paid her by Iggy, began to diminish. The long hours of hard work were still accompanied by kicks and blows but it seemed as though the captives were being gradually absorbed into the life of the tribe. Elly-May could see herself, in a matter of months, pregnant and wearing the same homespun dress and sandals as the other women. Even the attitude of the men seemed to be gradually changing, for although she still ranked as the lowest of the low, available at any time to any horny outlaw, it was the women taken from the Festival army who had suffered the gang rape during the victory celebrations. While she and Anna had still been passed from outlaw to outlaw until they were aching and exhausted, there had been no actual viciousness directed at them and one outlaw had even muttered drunkenly about taking her for his woman.

It seemed to Elly-May that she was gradually joining the tribe and it was about time she did something about it.

Returning from loading a box onto the supply wagon, she

met Anna struggling with a large bundle. Looking round to see that they were unobserved, they both stopped. Anna put down her bundle.

'You okay, kid? Las' night was kinda rough.'

'Yeah, I'm okay. I've knowed rougher nights onna strip.'

'Sure, but we useda get paid for 'em.'

'Lissen, wha' you think the chances are of givin' this place th' slip? Mebbe headin' north an' settin' up in business again? We could make f' one o' the iron towns.'

Anna thought for a moment.

'Wouldn' be easy unless we could nick some clothes. An' we'd havta watch out for tha' bitch Lucille, she'd blow th' whistle on us f' sure.'

'Might be easier once the men have moved out.'

'Mebbe. We better get movin', tha' ol' biddy in th' apron's watchin' us.'

Anna picked up her bundle and hurried off. Elly-May went back to the pile of provisions, still thinking through plans of escape.

As she came back from loading another bundle, a commotion behind her made her stop and turn. A crowd of tribeswomen were laughing and jeering, and in the middle of them two men held a struggling girl. Elly-May walked over for a better look. The girl was naked except for long white leather boots and a wide white belt. Two of the women were haggling over a red velvet cape that they had obviously just stripped from her. Torn between horror and sadistic amusement Elly-May watched as the two outlaws walked away and the women fell on the girl, beating and kicking her and fighting over her scanty but expensive garments.

Another of Iggy's castoffs was going through the nasty ritual.

*　　　*　　　*

Iggy fought to control his nervous crystal excitement as the army – his army – made ready to march. It was the fulfilment of his greatest ambition. He would lead the biggest army that the south had ever seen to the very walls of Festival.

Winston rode back and forth marshalling the men into compact groups, yelling for the troop leading to get their men into line. After some semblance of order had been achieved Iggy rode deliberately slowly to the head of the column. He shouted across to Winston.

'Okay kid, move 'em out.'

Winston turned in his saddle.

'Move out!'

The cry was echoed down the line.

'Move out!'

'Move out!'

Iggy clapped spurs to his horse and started down the highway; then like an enormous beast coming alive the outlaw army started out on its march to Festival.

*   *   *

Luther studied the backs of the two retainers as he plodded along the highway. After the rain of the previous day the sun had at first been welcome but by mid-afternoon the heat that beat upon his neck and was reflected from the road had become a tiresome nuisance.

The combination of sweat and his filthy clothes made him itch and his feet felt sore and blistered in boots made for riding rather than marching. To add to his discomfort the other two had not spoken to him since they had left the farmhouse, apparently blaming him for the escape of Valentine and the loss of the horse.

He found the simplest course was to put his brain in low gear and plod on mechanically, staring straight ahead. Problems like calculating the length of time it would take to reach Festival just added to his burden.

For a time he lagged a good thirty paces behind the other two; then he saw them stop and climb down the banking beside the highway to drink from a small stream.

They sat down and rummaged in their food bags. Luther climbed down too, but sat a little way off from the others. He munched on the bread and ham which he had brought from the farmhouse, occasionally drinking from the stream. A distant rumble made him look up but he was unable to see the highway from where he sat. The rumble came again and he climbed back up the bank to take a better look.

Shading his eyes against the afternoon sun, he looked back and gasped.

'Hey, hey yous guys. Take a look at this.'

The retainers looked up, resentful that Luther had broken the silence. He was standing on the highway above them pointing and shouting agitatedly.

'For fug's sake, c'mon an' look.'

Grudgingly they stuffed their uneaten food back into their bags and clambered up the bank to join him.

Almost on the horizon, like a dark smudge, a large body of men was coming towards them. The rumbling was almost continuous and beginning to distinguish itself as the sound of horses and marching men.

For a while they stood transfixed watching the smudge on the horizon grow larger and more solid. Then one of the retainers snapped into life.

'It's the fuggin' outlaws; we gotta get outta here.'

Luther turned round, looking for some kind of cover in the bare landscape. Further down the stream he spotted a clump of bushes and stunted trees.

'Them bushes, we can hide up there.'

The men scrambled down the slope, crashed through the stream and, after running along the opposite bank, flopped panting into the cover of the bushes.

For what seemed like an eternity the three of them lay listening to their heartbeats. The sound of the outlaw column grew louder and louder; then the first of them came into sight.

First came ranks of lean men on tall horses with repeating rifles and carbines; behind them rode a mass of stocky tribesmen on short-legged ponies. They were followed by lines of bowmen marching to the rhythm of a guttural call and response singing. Then came a massive steam engine, its iron wheels rumbling on the road surface and its enormous pistons rattling and clanking. In its wake marched a mob of foot soldiers armed with shotguns, axes or long pikes, and then even more horsemen, obviously freelancers by their varied styles and weapons. Finally a line of creaking supply wagons pulled by teams of mules brought up the rear.

The noise of the army faded into the distance. The three men from Festival crawled from the bushes where they had been hiding.

'Sweet prophet, didja see that!'

'Musta been more'n a thousand!'

'She-it!'

'I reckon tha's gotta be th' end o' Festival.'

White-faced, the three stared at each other.

'Reckon there's no use goin' back to Festival.'

'It'll be outlaw by this time tomorrow. They don' stand a chance.'

'I got a woman back in Festival!'

'Reckon you best f'get her. She'll be strapped to a rail with her legs spread b' time we get there.'

'Or worse.'

'Wha' the fug do we do?'

For a moment they all fell silent. Finally Luther spoke.

'Reckon I'll work me way north, mebbe hire on with an Iron Lord.'

He picked up his pack and the other two silently followed.

*   *   *

Elly-May and Anna lay huddled together on the earth floor pretending to sleep and listened to the breathing of the other captive women. When they felt that all were asleep, they tentatively sat up. The rhythm of breathing didn't alter and, one at a time, they crawled to the tent flap. Elly-

163

May opened it a fraction and peered out. She leaned over and breathed in Anna's ear:

'It looks like there's nobody about.'

Silently they slid through the flap.

Outside the remains of the evening fires made pinpoints of light and deep shadows. Some distance away one fire blazed brightly and the handful of men left to guard the town huddled round it. Elly-May and Anna carefully skirted the group of outlaws and picked their way towards the big tree at the edge of the highway where, while they were loading the wagons, they had hidden bundles containing food and clothes.

They were at the edge of the town and the tree was in sight when Elly-May felt Anna clutch at her arm.

'Whassamatta?'

Anna hissed her into silence and drew her down into the shadow of a tent. Silently Anna pointed and Elly-May saw two outlaws, obviously guards making their rounds, about to cross the space between them and the highway.

Scarcely daring to breathe, the two women crouched in the darkness, waiting for the guards to pass. They strolled closer and closer, and Elly-May was positive that they would hear her heart beating.

Not more than three paces from where the women lay, the two outlaws halted. There was a spark, a small flame and then a red glow as one of them lit a pipe. Elly-May could clearly hear every word of their conversation.

'Bad luck to draw camp guard while Festival falls.'

'Worse'n bad luck.'

'Aye. All tha' lootin' an' the women.'

The one with the pipe spat and passed it to his companion. Elly-May could see the pipe bowl glow bright as he inhaled. Then to her relief they started to walk on.

As soon as the outlaws were out of sight, the two women scrambled from their hiding place and dashed, barefoot, across the highway. After some fumbling in the dark they located their hidden bundles and quickly pulled on the leather tunics and sandals that they had stolen. Then, slinging the bags of food over their shoulders, they started down the highway, away from Afghan Promise, away from Festival and away from Iggy and his outlaw horde.

*　　　*　　　*

Winston looked around at the gathering dust and spurred his horse to catch up with Iggy at the head of the column.

'We gonna stop for the night? It's gonna be hard to see soonly.'

Iggy looked round at him as though Winston's voice had startled him out of deep, private thoughts.

'Wha'?'

'I said are we gonna pull up f' the night, it's gonna be dark soon.'

Iggy thought for a moment.

'Nah, march all night, that way we make Festival by mornin'.'

'We better make some kinda stop for eats.'

'Yeah, send out a coupla boys to scout out a place to stop. We'll take maybe two hours to rest, then move again. Okay?'

Winston looked dubious.

'Don'tcha think it's a mistake marchin' after dark?'

'We'll issue torches; nobody's gonna get lost.'

'I didn' mean that, I was jus' thinkin' 'bout how we gonna arrive at Festival wi' the men like dog tired.'

Iggy grinned at his second-in-command.

'Lissen buddy. When th' boys have fed, break out th' crystal. Then when they get to Festival they'll be crazy.'

XX

'They're comin',.'

'They're comin'.'

Joe Starkweather hurried to the ladder that led up the side of the Highway Gate watchtower and climbed it awkwardly. At the top Solly, one of the survivors of Valentine's attack on Afghan Promise, was peering agitatedly through a battered telescope.

'There's one helluva lotta them, Joe. Gotta be more'n even the scouts tol' us about on the road.'

'How many?'

'I dunno, looks like more'n a thousand t' me.'

'Let's have a look.'

Starkweather raised the telescope to his eye.

'Shit! You ain't kiddin'; there's maybe twelve hundred of them.'

He looked round grimly.

'It ain't gonna be easy. I'm goin' down to get the word out to the local commanders.'

*　　　*　　　*

A commotion in the courtyard attracted Valentine's attention and he moved to the window of the small palace room in which Starkweather's rebels had locked him.

Starkweather was standing in the middle of the palace yard surrounded by more of his gang. Obviously something was happening. Horsemen hurriedly came and went; the gates continuously opened and shut to let them in and out.

Valentine walked to the door and kicked it noisily.

'Guard! Guard! What's goin' on? Guard!'

After some moments the door opened and one of Starkweather's men stepped inside.

'Wha're you yellin' about?'

'What's goin' on out there?'

The guard thought for a moment.

'I s'pose there's no harm in you knowin'. The outlaws are outside the city.'

*　　*　　*

Iggy raised his hand and the outlaw army slowly came to a halt. He glanced round for Winston who manoeuvred his horse up next to Iggy.

'There seems to be some kinda barricade 'cross the highway.'

'Yeah, get th' puller moved up an' tell the horsemen from Oltha's tribe to form a line across th' road. Okay?'

'Ri'.'

Winston rode off to carry out Iggy's instructions. A while later there was a rumble as the huge traction engine rolled to the front of the column. Banana climbed down from the cab and hurried to where Iggy sat on his horse.

'Wha's gonna happen, boss?'

Iggy dismounted and led his horse to the side of the road as the cavalry that was once Oltha's hurried their stocky ponies to the front.

Iggy watched as they formed themselves into a long line across the width of the highway; then he turned to Banana.

'I'm gonna put half a dozen boys wi' rapid-fires up wi' you. You'll need the shields aroun' the cab. I wan' you to go in at full speed an' lose that barricade. The tribesmen'll follow you in. Okay?'

'Sho' chief; you wan' me to stay put or come back?'

'I wan' that barricade lost, then get back here quickly. Winston'll give you all th' details.'

*　　*　　*

Mac the Smith jumped down from the barricade.

'Here they come! They're usin' tha' fuggin' engine!'

167

He ran to his position on the line as the rest of the defenders scrambled for their weapons. There was some sporadic shooting and Mac swung round yelling.

'Okay, okay, don't fire; you gotta wait till they're in range. An' don't waste ammunition on that puller unless you can hit th' driver.'

The line of outlaw horsemen thundered nearer with the traction engine running out in front. Mac fought off the temptation to shoot wildly at it. He was sure that it would reach the barricade and probably smash through it. He crawled to the group of men next to him.

'Lissen, as soon as tha' puller hits try an' get up into the cab. It's our only chance of stoppin' it.'

'Okay Mac, we're wi' you.'

*   *   *

Banana crouched in the cab of the puller and manipulated the steering rods. Behind him were six of the boys tensely clutching their rapid-fires. The odd bullet clanged against the steel shielding mounted around the cab but for the most part the defenders seemed to be directing their fire at the horsemen.

'Better hol' onto somethin'; we gonna hit any minute.'

*   *   *

The engine hit the barricade with a splintering crash of shattered timber. It slowed but did not stop. The wagon that was the main part of that section was knocked out of the way while the smaller things, such as furniture and crates, were crushed under the machine's iron wheels.

Mac and his small group raced towards the puller as it cleared the barricade and began to turn in a wide curve. Desperately he looked for a clear shot at the driver but the entire cab was shrouded in steel shielding. A few paces in front of the others Mac broke into a sprint; his fingers clutched for the ladder that ran up to the cab. He managed

168

to grip the ladder with one hand and for a dozen paces he was dragged, running, across the highway. At last he was able to find a foothold on the ladder and slowly began to climb the swaying monster. Then the shielding above his head crashed open and there was a burst of machine-gun fire from the cab.

* * *

Banana laughed as Stan and Li'l Henry opened fire through the opening in the shields round the cab. A small group of Festival men were running towards the puller. All but one who clung to the cab ladder were cut down in the first burst. Stan leaned over the side of the cab and looked down at the man on the ladder, a working man with cropped head and muscular arms, who stared up at them as though transfixed. Stan fired a short burst and the man fell back onto the highway, his arms and legs flapping as he rolled.

Banana slowed down the puller and swung back another section of shielding. They were now behind the barricade and running parallel to it. He could see the first of the tribesmen swarming across it, grappling hand to hand with Festival men.

All six of the outlaws went to work on the defenders while Banana held the machine steady. It was yet another variation on Iggy's favourite crossfire trick: the men of Festival had no chance with the howling tribesmen on one side and the hail of bullets from the puller on the other. Banana noted that some of the tribesmen were hit by their fire but their companions seemed too crazed on crystal to notice or care.

Very soon the last defender had fallen. Banana swung the machine round and began picking up speed. Tribesmen leaped from their path as the puller butted a second hole in the barricade. Then they were rolling back down the highway to where Iggy waited.

* * *

Nasty Elaine and a handful of Northsiders stood their ground as the crowds of fleeing people rushed past. A hundred paces away, beside the highway, shacks and tents were burning. A couple of times, through the crowd, she had caught sight of outlaw horsemen on small shaggy ponies harassing the refugees running from their burning homes, but she had been unable to get a clear shot at them. Shotgun blasts had driven back a skirmishing party of outlaws on foot and it seemed that they were waiting for a larger force to move up before attempting to crush the last resistance of the Northside. They probably didn't realise, she thought bitterly, just how token that resistance would be. They had counted on being able to hold the outlaws, at least for a while, at the barricade and most of the weapons and ammunition had been sent there.

The last of the refugees streamed past and soon the central avenue of the Northside was empty except for the handful of men and women who crouched behind the ring of furniture, barrels and straw bales, waiting for the outlaw assault.

It was almost quiet. The muffled roar of the burning shacks and the occasional gunfire from the highway seemed a long way away.

Then outlaws came down the square like a breaking wave. They were not the same tribesmen on their squat ponies who had rushed the barricade: these were thin leather-clad men on tall horses. They swung heavy rapid-fire guns and had faces that seemed transformed by wild, evil lust.

Elaine swung up her shotgun and the first blast lifted one of them clear out of his saddle.

A second came at her: a slight, pale man with long, curly hair riding a huge black horse. She misjudged the shot and although his horse ploughed into the ground he rolled clear and jumped to his feet cursing and swinging his gun in her direction.

*   *   *

'Ya dirty bitch!'

The shock of his horse being shot from under him seemed to make Iggy's crystal-fed anger erupt into almost inhuman fury. His usual lazy, feminine face became a mask of hate. He jumped to his feet firing blindly. Then he saw the woman who had brought his horse down. She swung a shotgun by the barrel and was actually coming at him.

He squeezed the trigger and felt the machine gun buck in his hands. He went on firing long after the woman had fallen, watching her body twitch and jerk in the dust under the impact of the bullets.

Then his gun stopped as the clip ran out and he slowly lowered it. All round him the firing had ceased.

Winston pulled his horse to a stop beside him. Iggy looked up as though dazed when he spoke.

'You hurt?'

'No, no, jus' my horse totalled.'

'Everythin' north of the highway is ours now. You wan' we should set up camp here?'

Iggy looked around. His men sat on their horses waiting for orders.

'No, pull back onto th' highway f' the night. Tell the tribesmen t' burn this place to the ground.'

He paused.

'An' tell 'em they can do what they wan' with any prisoners. Oh, an' one other thing: tell 'em to start their dead singin' soon as it's dark. Tell 'em to sing loud an' long. Make sho' they don' get no sleep in Festival.'

XXI

'Is that hideous chant gonna go on all night?'

It was Frankie Lee's watch in front of the Last Chance. He pulled his cloak tighter around himself and shuddered. The chanting from out on the highway was getting to his head.

Claudette, who was sharing the watch with him, passed him a small jug of spirit.

'Here Frankie boy, have a hit on this.'

Frankie Lee tilted the jug, gave it back to Claudette and wiped his mouth.

'Like it says in me name text: "your loss will be my gain".'

For a while the two of them sat in silence; then the sound of footsteps made Frankie Lee stiffen and tighten his grip on the gun across his knees.

Slowly he stood up.

'Hold it right there!'

The footsteps stopped.

'Now come forward real nice an' slow.'

'Take it easy, Frankie, it's jus' me makin' the rounds.'

Frankie Lee recognised the voice of Joe Starkweather. The old man stepped into the porch of the Last Chance and sat down on the low wall of sandbags.

'Everythin' okay?'

'Sure, 'cept tha' godam singin'. It's givin' me the horrors.'

'It's only a hill tribe singin' the dead.'

Frankie Lee shook his head.

'Wha' they gotta do tha' for?'

'You never been in the hills?'

'Not as far out as you find the wild tribes. I'm a city kid.'

'After a hill tribe kills they sing a chant for the spirits of the dead. They believe it'll stop them seekin' revenge.'

'They gonna do that for us?'

'Who knows? Maybe we'll hold 'em, maybe we won't.'

'Northside couldn't hold 'em.'

'Like I said – who knows.'

Starkweather stood up.

'I gotta take a look at Shacktown. I'll see you people later.'

'Later, Mistuh Starkweather.'

They watched him disappear into the darkness and then sat in silence for a long while. It was Claudette who finally spoke.

'You think we're gonna die tomorrow?'

Frankie Lee looked at her and shrugged.

'Like Joe said – who knows.'

'You ain't as hard as you pretend, Frankie Lee. How come you didn' pull out wi' the other drifters?'

'Too much of a city kid, I s'pose.'

There was a long pause; then Claudette spoke again.

'I was real grateful tha' day y' took care o' me after th' whippin'.'

'Yeah?'

'I was wonderin' if'n mebbe you'd like to take a bottle back t' me room after we get off this watch.'

Frankie Lee smiled at her in the darkness.

'I'd like that jus' fine.'

*　　　*　　　*

The smell of the smoke from the burned section of the city and the eerie chanting of the tribesmen had made Valentine close the window, despite the fact that the room in which he was imprisoned was small and stuffy. For a long while he sat on the hard bed and stared vacantly in front of him. It was difficult to comprehend the changes that he had gone through in the previous two days. He had ridden out of the city at the head of a well armed and supposedly invincible force. Now he was a prisoner in his own palace. It was almost impossible to grasp.

Abruptly the chanting stopped and Valentine sprang to the window. Was it the start of a fresh assault? He could see very little from the high window. He pushed it open and listened carefully; everything seemed quiet. He stared down at the long drop to the courtyard below.

To his surprise he heard a voice whispering close beside him. He looked back into the room but it was still empty. Then it came again.

'My lord, my Lord Valentine.'

It was definitely coming from somewhere outside. Again he looked out of the window and saw a hand projecting from a window on the same floor.

'My lord, can you hear me?'

Valentine slid his head through the narrow space.

'Who is that?'

'It's me, my lord, Preach. There's five of us boys in here. They locked us in here when we wouldn't go along wi' their comnie plans.'

'So you're prisoners?'

'Tha's right, my lord.'

'I don't really see how you can be of any use to me.'

'We're your loyal servants, my lord, tha's why they locked us up.'

'You're nonetheless locked up.'

'We thought there might be a chance of breakin' out in th' confusion of the outlaw attacks. Given the right opportunity, we might even seize the palace back from th' cursed comnies an' restore you, my lord, to your ri'ful place.'

'You think there's a chance of that?'

'Certainly, my lord. As the outlaws cause more trouble, Starkweather an' his crew have less an' less time to pay attention to us.'

Hope rose inside Valentine, maybe all was not lost. Maybe he would, after all, regain his title. Once he was in control of the palace, the outlaws were only a minor problem.

*　　　*　　　●

Soon after the night's drinking had begun, Iggy had slipped away from Winston's attentive eye and walked, on his own, out of the camp on the highway.

Flames still danced around the embers of the northern section of the city and the smoke drifted across the highway towards him, occasionally stinging his eyes and throat as a billow engulfed him. For a while he stood beside the shattered barricade and noted that the dead had been removed in the time since he had withdrawn his men. It was Starkweather all over: methodical down to the last detail.

He walked through one of the gaping holes in the barricade and on down the highway. The walls of Festival loomed above him and beyond them he could see the lights in the top windows of the palace. He smiled in the darkness, if only they knew that he was out here alone. One bullet could save their whole city.

After a while he turned on his heel and walked towards the still burning ruins. Bodies still littered the area and it was only the heat from the smouldering rubble that kept the rats at bay.

He picked his way down the broad main avenue, sticking fairly closely to the middle, as many of the ruins were still too hot to approach.

He heard a sound to his left and froze. Carefully he slid his gun from its holster and dropped to one knee. Holding the gun in front of him he slowly pivoted, scanning the surrounding piles of debris. The sound came again faintly.

'Help me, help me.'

The voice sounded very weak and Iggy thought he detected a slight movement at the base of a heap of collapsed timbers in roughly the direction from which the sound had come. Slowly he stood up and, gun in hand, walked towards the source of the sound.

A man lay pinned by a large beam, the shoulder of his shirt was caked with drying blood. He was conscious and obviously in serious pain. Iggy stood over the man and dropped his gun back into its holster. The man gestured weakly.

175

'For pity's sake help me.'

A grin crossed Iggy's face.

'Why?'

'Help me, please. Help me get this beam off me.'

'I wanna know why. Some reason why I should take th' trouble to help you.'

'But I'll die, I'll die if you leave me here. You can't let me die.'

'Why not? I organised the manner of your death inna firs' place.'

The man's eyes widened in fear.

'You're an outlaw.'

'No longer. I am Iggy, the new lord of Festival. You are my subject an' godam slow at answerin' my question.'

'Question?'

'The question why I should bother t' help you in your current troubles.'

The man became desperate.

'But I'll die, I'll die!'

Iggy frowned impatiently.

'You already said that. It's no valid reason. I'm still waitin'. For anyone who seems so hung up you don' try so very hard.'

'But just for human pity, mercy, call it what you like.'

'Pity? Mercy? I never noticed that Festival was so strong on mercy or pity, wi' your floggin's an' your hungry. I don' think that'll really do. I reckon I'm gonna leave you jus' as you are.'

'At least finish me. Shoot me an' end the pain.'

'I don't really think tha's possible. I'd attract too much attention.'

The man sobbed as Iggy walked into the darkness.

*　　　*　　　*

'So if'n we don' run 'em off tomorrow, tha's it?'

'It would seem so.'

Old Tom and Joe Starkweather sat in the kitchen of the

176

palace, both men looking grim and tired.

'How much ammunition we got lef'?'

'Enough for one day's fightin' if they attack all three sections in force, which they mos' likely will. We could maybe hold the palace for another day. There's so many of them.'

'It looks bad.'

'Yeah. Unless we can get Iggy an' his lieutenants. That could maybe break up the attack.'

'When d'you figure they'll come?'

'Not before dawn, the hill tribes won't fight in the dark.'

Old Tom stared into his drink for long moments. Wearily he looked at Starkweather.

'So wha' happens here tomorrow?'

'I want you to take care of this section. I've arranged with Frankie Lee an' the Kid to run up a signal if they can't hold the attackers an' I'll take what horsemen we got an' try an' cover 'em so their people can get back in here. The only thing you gotta worry about is havin' a crew on the gate that can get it open an' shut real fast.'

'I'll make sure of that, don' worry.'

XXII

Banana surfaced from a deep sleep to find Winston shaking him. He rubbed his eyes and looked around. Inside the tent it was still dark.

'Whassamatta?'

'Iggy wants you, you better get up.'

'It's the middle of th' fuggin' night.'

'It's jus' before dawn, so get up.'

Banana rolled out of his blankets and stood up yawning.

'Wha's th' trouble then?'

'Iggy'll tell you when we get there.'

He pulled on his boots and jacket and followed Winston through the still slumbering camp. To the east, beyond the city, the sky was a lighter shade of grey.

Two armed guards stood outside Iggy's tent and one of them held back the flap as Winston and Banana ducked inside. Iggy sprawled in the chair that had once belonged to Oltha. He nursed a bottle of spirit and looked as though he had not slept. He glanced up as the two men entered the tent.

'Looks like this is the big day, we should have the whole city by nightfall.'

Banana grinned.

'Good times tonight, huh boss? Get us them Festival women?'

Iggy grinned.

'Sho' nuff kid, but we got work to do ri' now.'

'Sho' boss.'

'How long you need to get that puller goin'?'

Banana thought for a moment.

'Shouldn' take too long; there's plenty wood. Maybe an hour at th' outside.'

'Good, then start it happenin'.'

'Okay chief.'

Banana ducked out of the tent.

'An' Winston.'

'Yeah.'

'You better start wakin' up the camp.'

*   *   *

Claudette's body was warm against Frankie Lee as they lay together in the narrow bed. It was tempting to shut his eyes and go back to sleep but the knowledge of the outlaws outside the city forced him into wakefulness.

Claudette mumbled in her sleep as he slid out of bed and padded naked to the window. He swung open the shutter a little and looked outside. The sky was lightening and the city was quiet, nothing moving in the empty avenue. Only the pall of smoke to the north belied the peaceful appearance.

He looked back at Claudette who had rolled over on her stomach and lay sprawled across the bed. Although they were fading, the marks of the flogging still showed as parallel stripes across her back.

He walked back to the bed and sat down. Softly he kissed her ear.

'Wake up babe, it's dawn.'

Sleepily she rolled over.

'Wha'?'

'It's dawn babe, we oughta be movin'.'

She opened her eyes and pouted.

'Already?'

' 'Fraid so.'

'Aw, c'mon back t' bed f' a while.'

'We oughta be gettin' over to th' Chance.'

'They can wait a while; c'mon back here.'

She ran fingernails lightly across his stomach.

'C'mon.'

*   *   *

The puller rolled slowly down the highway. Crowded behind it were a horde of foot soldiers staying close to the machine, ready to use it as cover if fired upon. Behind them, some way back, Iggy sat motionless in front of a mass of horsemen who spread out over the entire highway.

The puller moved slowly forward, allowing the men on foot to keep pace with it. Heads appeared on the walls of Festival but no shots were fired. The only sound was the clank and rumble of the machine and the shuffle of the men moving forward.

They passed the barricade, and the sun resting on the horizon caused the tall engine to cast a long shadow over the men following it.

Gradually it began to pick up speed and then, at the side road that led to the Merchants' Quarter, it abruptly swung to the right and raced down the incline that led to the high fence and wooden gates. The men on foot became strung out behind, running to keep up.

A few shots were fired from the Quarter walls but these had no effect on the steel-shielded machine. As it raced towards the walls it showed no sign of braking or slackening speed. Some defenders leaped from the firing gallery to avoid the inevitable impact while others remained, firing futilely at the oncoming giant.

There was an awful rending crash as the machine hit. The gate fell backwards and a length of wooden wall collapsed. The puller swung into a tight turn, attempting to repeat the trick of the day before as the attackers on foot raced towards the gap. Halfway through the manoeuvre the machine appeared to falter. Inside the cab, Banana fought with the steering rods. For a long moment it appeared to hang poised on two wheels, then ponderously it began to topple.

It fell on its side with a crash of anguished metal. The shields dropped from the cab and men burst from it firing. Defenders rushed to surround the wreck. Banana found himself grappling hand to hand with a burly retainer.

Then the boiler blew.

The noise was so intense that it was felt as a pain rather than heard. Steam rocketed in every direction, both sides stood frozen as the echoes faded and were replaced by the screams of scalded, dying men.

The moment passed, the air was filled with the thunder of hooves and yelling of warriors as Iggy's entire cavalry charged down the highway.

*   *   *

They boiled into the Merchants' Quarter shooting and hacking. The terrified population ran around like ants whose nest has been stirred with a stick. Some tried to save possessions while others attempted to resist the invaders, but for the most part they simply ran up and down the avenues trying to avoid the howling outlaws.

Leaving the tribesmen and the freelancers to rampage freely, Iggy and his original seventy headed straight down the central avenue, straight for the South Gate. A handful of retainers ran from the gate house but were cut down by the leading horsemen.

At the gate Iggy swung his men round and, leaving a group to see that the gate would not be opened, he ordered the others to spread out. Systematically they moved back through the Quarter either killing or driving all before them back towards the milling, slaughtering hill men.

*   *   *

High up on the west wall of Backstage, Joe Starkweather and a group of his men stared down at the butchery in the Merchants' Quarter. Horrified, a young guard swung round to Starkweather.

'Why the fug don' we open fire? Those people are gettin' massacred.'

'Hold your fire an' shut up!'

'But . . .'

'Those people have the guns an' ammunition that could

have defended all of us. I don' intend using the little we have to get them off the hook.'

'You're as bad as them fuggin' outlaws.'

Starkweather grabbed the kid by the shoulders.

'Listen punk, we don't have enough to defend ourselves without pumpin' half of it down there. They opted out an' there's nothin' we can do. So get a grip on yourself an' get back to your post.'

The young trooper shook his head and stumbled away. Starkweather grimly watched him go and then turned back to the battle below him.

*   *   *

Frankie Lee looked round the circle of tense faces.

'They're inside the Merchants' Quarter an' there's a good chance they'll come outta the South Gate an' straight at us. If that happens it's down to us to hold 'em long enough f' the boys in the trenches t' either get back here or to Lou's. If one o' the houses falls on 'em it's also down to the people in th' other one to give enough coverin' fire f' them to get across the Drag. If both houses start to go we fire the flare an' Joe'll cover us so's we can get behind the walls. Everyone clear?'

The defenders who were crowded inside the bar of the Last Chance nodded silently.

'Okay then, you all best get t' your positions.'

*   *   *

The Merchants' Quarter had fallen. Some of the buildings around the North Gate were on fire but for the most part it remained intact. Of the population only a few survived: the tiny minority who had managed to flee over the walls and a handful of young women who were already being herded back to the outlaw camp surrounded by leering guards. It was becoming apparent that Iggy's war on Festival was one of complete attrition. In Shacktown and on the Drag the defenders waited while he organised his next move.

With his advantage of arms and numbers Iggy saw no need to hurry. The Festival men would never chance coming out from behind their defences and pushing a counter attack; time was completely on his side.

Almost casually he cantered his horse down the avenue where Winston had lined up the entire force. He reined in beside Winston.

'Cut out half of the mounted tribesmen; I'll take them an' our boys outta the South Gate an' hit th' Drag. You take the resta the bunch an' circle roun' the walls. We'll meet up in the arena.'

Iggy sat on his horse and watched as Winston rode up and down, yelling, cursing and gesticulating, dividing the outlaws into the two groups. When it was finally accomplished he rode back to Iggy.

'There y' go boss, you wan' me to move 'em out?'

'Jus' hold on a while.'

He urged his horse forward and looked around at the assembled outlaws.

'Okay yous guys, we're gonna clean up th' resta this city. Half o' yous'll take Shacktown an' th' other half'll come wi' me an' clean up th' Drag. After that we link up an' hit them walls.'

He gestured at the high Backstage that loomed behind him. There was a hysterical tone creeping into his voice.

'An' after they fall, tha's when the party starts!'

His voice rose to a scream:

'OKAY?'

There was a roar of assent from the outlaw rank. Iggy swung his horse round, jerking the reins so it pranced and reared. As he galloped towards the South Gate his men fell in behind him, whooping and yelling.

*   *   *

As the sound of the footsteps of the guard bringing the

midday meal came faintly through the door, Preach backed up against the wall. He motioned the others to silence.

'Jus' sit there an' act natural, I'll take care o' the rest.'

The keys rattled in the lock and the door swung open. It opened inwards and hid Preach, pressed against the wall, from the guard.

'Here's the food, lads.'

The trooper stooped and set the tray on the floor. As he straightened, a puzzled frown crossed his face.

'Hey! Where's th' other ...'

His words were cut short as Preach's clasped hands struck at the back of his neck. The trooper slumped to the floor. Preach snatched the gun and keys from the guard and slipped through into the corridor. He beckoned to the others.

'Okay, it's clear.'

The other men followed him out of the room. Halfway down the corridor, Preach halted.

'This is th' lord's room.'

He banged on the door.

'My lord, my Lord Valentine. It's me, Preach. We come to get you out.'

There was a muffled reply from inside the room.

'My lord, please stand back, I'm gonna blow the lock off.'

One of the other men caught Preach by the arm.

'If you shoot you'll have Starkweather's fuggin' guards down on us.'

Preach shook him off.

'We'll take care o' that, an' mind your language, th' lord might hear you.'

He put the gun to the lock and pulled the trigger. The explosion was deafening in the small corridor. Preach put his shoulder to the door and pushed. It swung open. Valentine stood in the centre of the room. He looked pale and unshaven and stood blinking at the men.

'So you're my loyal troops, are you? You're a sorry looking lot.'

184

The five troopers shuffled uncomfortably. Preach scratched his ear.

'We been locked up f' some time, my lord.'

Valentine stepped into the corridor and glanced round.

'How many guns you got?'

'Jus' one, my lord.'

'Give it to me.'

Preach handed over the gun.

'Wha' do we do now, my lord?'

Valentine started down the corridor.

'Follow me.'

As they reached the end of the corridor a sound made them turn.

'The guard! He's woken up!'

Valentine pushed past the men. The guard leaned against the wall shaking his head. Valentine raised the gun carefully and fired. The guard twisted and hit the ground. The men stared, open mouthed.

'He's dead. We knowed him, we rode with him.'

Valentine stared at them with contempt.

'Shut up an' follow me.'

XXIII

The South Gate of the Merchants' Quarter flew open and Iggy's horsemen thundered in. The men in the trenches broke and ran; a few were cut down but most made the shelter of either Madame Lou's or the Last Chance. Frankie Lee crouched on the sandbagged porch of the Chance directing the heavy rapid-fire at the first wave of horsemen who, under the hail of bullets from the two houses, crashed into a confusion of plunging horses and falling men.

Frankie Lee looked round in jubilation as the outlaws withdrew towards the Merchants' Quarter to regroup.

'We broke the charge, we stopped 'em.'

Harry Krishna pointed.

'Looks like they're up t' somethin', Frankie.'

The outlaws were bunched, out of range, in front of the Merchants' Quarter. Men on foot hurried out of the gate carrying bundles, and wisps of smoke rose from the ranks. Ace looked at Frankie Lee.

'Wha' they up to?'

As if in answer a handful of riders detached themselves from the main group and galloped towards the Drag. In their hands they carried blazing torches.

'Fire! They're tryin' to burn us out!'

'Pick 'em off before they reach the buildings.'

The defenders opened fire and two of the outlaws immediately crashed into the dust. The other kept on coming. More went down but two managed to reach the end of the street and, before they were shot down, hurled their torches at one of the abandoned buildings.

The dry timbers with their many coats of paint blazed quickly, flames licking hungrily up the side of the house. Frankie Lee cursed as thick smoke rolled across the Drag, obscuring the approaches from the South Gate.

'Should we try an' put out th' fire?'

'No way, stay put, you wouldn't last a minute in the open. Watch the street, they're gonna be comin' through that smoke any minute.'

As though in reply the first outlaw broke through the smoke, crouched low in his saddle and firing as he came. More followed, strung out in a long line to make less effective targets for the machine gun. They streamed down the Drag firing alternately left and right and although many went down the majority made it down the street and out into the Arena where they turned in a wide circle and headed back towards the South Gate.

When they had passed Frankie Lee looked round. Harry Krishna and two other men lay groaning on the porch. He signalled to the defenders inside the bar.

'Get these men inside an' try an' make 'em comfortable.'

Men hurried from inside bearing crude stretchers. Frankie turned to the ones still standing.

'Nex' time they come, aim f' the horses we gotta snarl up that line. We ain't got the ammunition t' try an' pick 'em off as they run round us.'

He followed the stretcher bearers into the bar and watched as Claudette and one of the barmen busied themselves with the wounded.

'They gonna be okay?'

Claudette looked up.

'Al's dead, an' I don' reckon Nick or Harry's gonna last much longer.'

Before Frankie could reply there was a shout from outside.

'They're comin' again!'

Frankie Lee burst through the door, firing as he hit the porch. Bullets crashed into the woodwork behind him and he threw himself flat. The outlaws streamed past, firing as they went. By the time he had crawled to the sandbags they had passed and two more men lay dead on the porch. Ace looked at him anxiously.

'They're whittlin' us down, Frankie. We got mebbe a dozen of 'em that time but it's costin' us.'

'Yeah I know, best we move back inside before the nex' pass. We're too easy a target out here.'

*   *   *

After the third wild rush down the Drag, Iggy halted beside the South Gate and gathered his top guns around him.

'We're gonna hafta be suss about this. The boys in those cat houses are tough, we're hurtin' 'em, but we're losin' too many men. I'm gonna send down one more charge wi' the hill boys in front an' us followin'. Only this time it's gonna be different. Soon as you boys reach the firs' buildin', hit the ground an' beat it f' cover. Then work your way down th' street an' try to get inside one o' them houses. Concentrate on th' one on the left, th' one wi' the sign that says Madame Lou's. Ri'?'

The outlaws nodded. Iggy turned his horse and rode to where the tribesmen were gathered, their painted faces smeared with sweat.

'I'm gonna give you a great honour. Yous can lead the nex' charge. We aim f' the house on the right. You understand?'

The head gun, once Oltha's deputy, raised his rifle.

'We understand.'

'It would be lastin' shame to the tent of any warrior who lives but doesn' reach that house.'

Again the head gun raised his weapon.

'None will turn back!'

Iggy smiled.

'I'm real glad 'bout that. Okay, lead your men out.'

*   *   *

Ace and Frankie Lee stared through adjacent firing slits in the boarded windows.

'They're a long time comin'. Reckon they've called it off.'

Frankie Lee shook his head.

188

'They'll be back.'

He turned from the slit and looked round the room. It had come a long way from the dim, smoky, comfortable bar room that he had hung out in for so long. It was still dim and still smoky but the pleasant fog of booze and weed had been replaced by the acrid bite of gunpowder. The dark stained timbers were no longer friendly but seemed to brood on fear and menace, the furniture that had been broken to bar doors and stop windows seemed to be a symbol of the coming destruction. Frankie Lee had always liked the way sunlight slanted through the haze of the daytime bar room but now the shafts of smoky light seemed filled with bright menace.

There was a trace of despair in the faces of all his companions as they gripped their weapons and waited out the lull. The pile of ammunition stacked in the centre of the room was getting alarmingly small.

The room was silent; the only sounds came from outside: the crackle of the burning building, distant screams and gunfire coming from Shacktown.

Claudette looked up from where she was doing her best to care for the wounded.

'Harry Krishna's dead.'

*   *   *

The tribesmen, yelling and howling, raced into the smoke of the Drag. Iggy held his own men back for a few more moments as the chatter of rapid-fire preceded a chorus of screams from men and horses. Iggy smiled, put the tribesmen under threat of shame and they would willingly commit suicide.

'Okay!'

Iggy urged his men forward, following the tribesmen with a good deal more caution.

As they broke through the pall of smoke, a spectacle of carnage met their eyes. Dead men and horses were littered all over the street. Small groups crouched behind their fallen horses and were firing into the Last Chance while others made futile rushes at the building, which invariably ended with the fast hammering of the rapid-fire.

A man immediately in front of Iggy screamed and toppled from his horse. It was time to move. Iggy signalled to the outlaws behind him and slid from his horse, hitting the dust and rolling to avoid the oncoming hooves. A dozen of his men followed suit.

Crouching and weaving he ran for the cover of a deserted house. For a moment he lay gasping in the shadow of the building as one by one the rest of his team joined him.

'This ain't no suicide deal. We gonna get into that house an' we gonna walk out, so take care, let the hill boys be brave, jus' work y' way down th' street nice an' easy. We'll meet up this side o' Madame Lou's. An' remember, don' let them fuggers inna Chance get a shot at yous. Ri'?'

'Ri'.'

One at a time the outlaws slipped away, carefully working their way down the Drag in quick dashes from building to building.

*   *   *

'They're crazy! They jus' keep comin'!'

Despite their terrible losses, the tribesmen kept attempting to rush the front of the Last Chance. Ace looked at Frankie Lee; he was obviously close to panic.

'We musta killed hundreds! Why don' they pull back?'

'They gotta be under threat of shame. It makes 'em a suicide squad. Jus' keep shootin'.'

Although he tried to conceal it from Ace, Frankie Lee was worried. Iggy might be crazy but he wouldn't waste so many men and horses unless he was up to something.

*   *   *

'Here's the plan.'

Iggy crouched with his men grouped around him in the shadow of Madame Lou's.

'The difficulty is that we're gonna hafta work our way along the front o' th' place an' break through the front door wi'out drawin' fire from across th' street.'

*   *   *

A stocky tribesman sprang with a yell onto the front porch of the Last Chance and rushed to the front door waving a heavy war axe but before he could land the first blow Big Red's shotgun knocked him off his feet.

Suddenly Ace yelled.

'There's men tryin' to break into Lou's place.'

Frankie Lee swung his gun in the direction of the cat-house door.

*   *   *

Iggy hit the ground and rolled as bullets kicked up the dust at his feet and thudded into the woodwork beside him. Paddy and Eugene worked on the barricaded door with their gun butts. It was impossible for the defenders to get a clear shot at them but the men in the Last Chance had seen them. Iggy screamed to the tribesmen.

'At them, at them! Stop those fuggin' guns!'

Eugene spun and fell but Finger leaped into his place. A group of tribesmen rushed at the Last Chance, giving Iggy and his men some cover, until they were shot down.

The barricaded door gave way and the outlaws' rapid-fires started their cruel hammering as the outlaws blasted their way inside.

*   *   *

'They're inside Lou's, they've busted the door in.'

'Frankie! There ain't too much ammunition left.'

The last rush from the street had drained most of their

remaining stocks but it had also broken the back of the hill men's attack. Only a handful remained, most of them retreating to the line of outlaws who fired sporadically from the end of the street.

One-Legged Terry burst from the door of Madame Lou's and hopped awkwardly across the Drag towards the shelter of the Last Chance. In the middle of the street he was shot down by an outlaw who appeared in the doorway.

Frankie Lee took a shot at him but missed. Before he could let go a second round, the man had ducked out of sight.

*   *   *

From a high window on the top floor of Madame Lou's Iggy looked down on the Drag, comparatively quiet since the remains of the hill tribes had drawn back. The street was littered with dead and wounded. Those fuggers had cost him a lot of men but he could afford to lose tribesmen.

It was a pity that his men had had to kill the women inside Madame Lou's: they would have been useful at the victory celebration but they had fought like wild animals and capture had been impossible.

He turned to the four men beside him and pointed to the Last Chance.

'See that window, th' one on the right of the door?'

'Wha' 'bout it?'

'Tha's th' one wi' the rapid-fire behind it. If we can fire together the boards'll cave in an' we'll be able to pin 'em down while th' rest of the boys move in.'

*   *   *

A hail of bullets smashed into the window and the wood splintered and cracked. Ace fell back, blood pouring from his throat.

Frankie Lee hit the floor and rolled out of reach of the shattering hail of bullets.

'They're firin' from the top windows.'

Huey yelled from the other side of the room.

'There's more of 'em movin' up th' street.'

Frankie Lee sprang to his feet. The barrage of firing still crashed into the front of the building and it was impossible to reach the fire slits. He rammed the last clip into the rapid-fire.

'Red, you better leggo the signal, we gotta get outta here.'

XXIV

The gate swung back and Joe Starkweather rode out into the arena with twenty mounted men behind him. In tight formation they galloped out into the arena.

As they swung towards the Drag, shouts from the direction of Shacktown caused Starkweather to turn in his saddle. Emerging from the burning ruins were a large force of outlaws.

In a flash, the elation of Killer Joe riding at the head of his men once again disappeared.

Grimly he reined in beside his second-in-command.

'Stay here with half the men. I'll head for the Drag an' try an' get those boys out from the Last Chance. If you can't hold that bunch, beat it back behind the walls.'

*   *   *

Frankie Lee shot two outlaws who appeared in the shattered door. Beside him, Claudette brought down another who had attempted to swing his gun through one of the gaping windows. The remaining defenders left in the Last Chance were now crouched behind the broken furniture, trying desperately to stop the outlaws from entering the building.

Two more outlaws bust through the doorway and managed to loose some wild shots before Frankie Lee was able to cut them down with a burst from his rapid-fire.

Another outlaw leaped into the room and Frankie Lee again pulled the trigger but this time nothing happened. The final clip was empty. Before he could draw his pistol the outlaw had fired and searing pain told him that the bullet had taken him in the arm. He dropped to his knees as the man raised his carbine to fire again. Then Claudette's shotgun roared and the outlaw fell.

Frankie climbed weakly to his feet, his left arm throbbing painfully. Another of Iggy's men came at him swinging a long knife. Using his good arm he smashed the man in the ribs with his empty gun. The man crashed to the floor with a grunt. Frankie Lee dropped the rapid-fire and pulled out his pistol. Before the man could climb to his feet he shot him.

More outlaws poured through the door but two suddenly crumpled to the floor. The others swung round. Shouts and firing came from outside, then Joe Starkweather and three other Festival men backed through the doorway, firing into the street.

'Okay Frankie Lee, move your people out. We're coverin' for you.'

*   *   *

Isaac Feinberg crouched in the sound shack on the side of the Stage and watched the small group of Festival horsemen struggling to hold back the outlaws who flooded out of Shacktown.

It was looking more and more like the death of Festival, and Feinberg had resigned himself to his own passing.

A sound outside the shack caught Feinberg's attention. The outlaws surely couldn't have reached the Stage. The next moment the door burst open and three soldiers in grimy palace colours crowded into the small equipment-filled room.

'Isaac Feinberg?'

'Yes.'

'You are ordered to play th' final text.'

'What? Now? Who gave that ridiculous order? I don't believe Joe gave any such order, it'd undermine morale completely an' things are bad enough already.'

'The order was given by Valentine, lord of Festival.'

'Valentine?'

'The lord has regained his ri'ful authority.'

'Preserve us all!'

'Play th' text.'

'All right, all right. You'll have to wait while I warm up the equipment.'

'Hurry!'

Feinberg busied himself with his gear and small red lights blossomed into life. After a while the monitor speaker began to hum and crackle.

'You brought the text?'

Silently the trooper handed Feinberg a worn black disc. Feinberg placed it on the turntable and dropped the pickup arm.

'This is the end, beau-ti ful friend.'

Morrizen, the lizard king, one of the great witch kings of the crowded years of legend that preceded the disaster. Second only to the terrible Djeggar. Morrizen, who had taken his words of doom to his unmarked grave, roared

'. . . in a des-p'rate land.'

Rough hands seized Feinberg and he was dragged out onto the stage and forced to his knees. Valentine's men faced him, the PA forcing them to yell in order to be heard above the Morrizen's text.

'Lost in a Ro-man wil-der-ness of pain,
and all the chil-dren are in-sane;'

'Feinberg, it's evidenced tha' you're associate an' conspirator wi' the renegade Starkweather.'

Feinberg tried to speak but he was drowned out by the sound.

'The snake is long, sev-en miles.'

'The penalty f' this is summary execution, you can make no appeal.'

'The West is the best.'

As the trooper raised his gun, Feinberg spread his hands in resignation.

*　　*　　*

The text rang over the arena, even above the noise of battle. Mounted behind Starkweather, Frankie Lee clung to Joe's back as the Festival troop raced for the gate only paces ahead of the outlaws. His arm was bleeding and he had difficulty staying on the horse as he grew weaker and dizzier.

They had been lucky. The text, unexpectedly roaring from the Stage, had thrown the outlaws into confusion as the tribesmen were filled with superstitious fear. It had given the Festival men time to regroup in the middle of the arena and to cut through the outlaws in a dash for the arena.

Dimly, through a haze of pain, Frankie Lee realised that the gates were not opening as they approached. In front of them Starkweather jumped from his horse and beat on the gate.

'C'mon you fuggin' idiots! Open the godam gate!'

The peephole in the gate slid out and a face appeared. Valentine's voice came from within. It was cold with a brittle overtone of insanity.

'The gate stays shut, Starkweather. You'll never come inside these walls again.'

The peephole slammed shut and Frankie Lee saw Starkweather, white-faced and looking very old, turn to face the onrushing outlaws. Then weakness and loss of blood overcame him and he sank into a dark oblivion.

XXV

Gradually Frankie Lee returned to painful consciousness. His wounded arm throbbed dully and a heavy weight pressed into his chest. He opened his eyes and found himself staring at a darkening sky. The corpse of an outlaw lay across his chest. It was quiet and obviously the fighting had ceased. As he cautiously turned his head to the left, the Arena Gate swam into his vision and the memory of the last moments in front of the gate returned. Valentine's crazy voice, Starkweather demanding entrance and the physical shock of the outlaw cavalry smashing into them, all flooded back to him.

He forced his eyes to focus and saw that the great wooden gate lay open and shattered, surrounded by bodies. Grimly he realised that if the outlaws who stood around the gate laughing and passing round looted jugs of spirit saw that he was alive, he would be shot where he had fallen.

For a while he lay still, scarcely daring to breathe. The sun was going down over the fallen city and perhaps he would have a chance to escape when it grew dark. He saw that the men by the gate were paying no attention to the scattered bodies and, cautiously, he ventured turning his head to the right. In front of him was the whipping post, tied to it hung the horribly mutilated body of Valentine. At least there was satisfaction in knowing that the pig had got his.

A little way off stood a group of outlaws who, from the attitude of others who came and went, seemed to be in authority. One of them turned in Frankie Lee's direction and in a flash of recognition he realised that it was Iggy, the outlaw leader. Anger flared like a spark of life in his shattered body. He was so close to the man who had caused the death of all his friends and destroyed the only place he had ever called home. He was so close but there was nothing he could do.

The weight of the dead outlaw seemed to be pressing something hard against his stomach. Gingerly, with the minimum of apparent movement, he slid his hand under the corpse and along his own body. His fingers touched metal.

The gun!

He still had the pistol, the one he had scored from the rube in what now seemed a different age. Maybe there was a chance he could even the score.

*　　*　　*

Iggy stared over the ruins of Festival. Now that the city was his he felt strangely deflated. The sense of power that had been so strong during the fighting had totally left him. Despite the crystal he had taken he felt drained and tired; the prospect of reconstruction and of organising his kingdom filled him with a weary reluctance to do anything. Even Winston's solid enthusiasm was becoming irksome. He shrugged: he was probably coming down.

He turned and walked towards a group of men who clustered laughing and drinking beside the Arena Gate. Winston and his bodyguards fell into step behind.

*　　*　　*

None of the outlaws seemed to be looking in his direction and Frankie Lee decided to take a chance on moving. He managed to wriggle slowly forward until the corpse was draped across his legs as he lay on his back with his hand, holding the gun, hidden beneath him. He froze as Iggy and his entourage walked past only a few paces from him. He watched Iggy halt among the men at the gate. They all had their backs to him and, although the light was fading fast, there was still enough to shoot by. It seemed to be his chance.

He pulled his legs free of the dead man and rolled onto

his side. Steadying the gun with both hands he took careful aim.

* * *

Winston watched Iggy as he joked with the men standing around the shattered gate. He was looking rough. Three days without food or sleep, surviving on straight crystal, would soon make their mark on him in the form of a prolonged comedown of which withdrawal and tiredness were the first signs. Iggy's comedowns were never pleasant for those around him.

Winston fretted at Iggy's unwillingness to do anything. There was the problem of the dead. Most of the men would be unwilling to do anything but party for the next few days but if the bodies were not quickly cleared, rats, wild dogs and finally plague would overrun the city.

The shot took him completely by surprise. At first he assumed that it was one of the men either celebrating or fighting. It was only when Iggy pitched forward that he realised it was an attempt to kill his chief.

Drawing his own gun he swung round staring into the darkness for some sign of the assassin.

'There! Runnin'!'

One of the men beside him shouted and fired. A dark shape was racing along the wall heading desperately for the ruins of the Merchants' Quarter. Winston fired a burst from his gun but the figure was an impossible target, alternately silhouetted against the flames and invisible in the black shadows they cast, then it seemed to vanish in the burning ruins.

One of the men kneeling over Iggy looked up, his face white with shock.

'He's dead!'

Turning towards the Merchants' Quarter, Winston broke into a run.

Two men crouched beside Iggy's body while the rest took off after Winston.

* * *

Frankie Lee felt sick and dizzy but he stumbled on. At first he had run blindly, expecting to be shot down at any time, but once he had reached the ruins he realised that there might be a chance that he could actually escape.

His arm throbbed painfully and his knees were dangerously weak. It was pointless in his condition to try and run from the pursuers who crashed through the ruins behind him. He looked around for a place to hide. A narrow space under a fallen wall, just big enough for a man to crawl inside, seemed ideal. Quickly he dropped to his hands and knees and wriggled into the gap. Gratefully he lay down in the darkness and waited.

*   *   *

Walking with a start he realised that he must have drifted into unconsciousness. There was no way of knowing whether he had been out for minutes or hours. He peered out from his hiding place. Everything was quiet and it looked much darker. It was probable that he had lain there for hours. His arm and shoulder hurt like hell as he crawled out of the hole in the ruins and for a moment he crouched on the ground, biting his lip until the pain subsided. Then he stood up and looked round, taking stock of his situation.

There was little point in heading west, the outlaws held the highway at least as far as Afghan Promise. His best bet was to work his way through the Northside, then strike out along the highway for the eastern villages beyond the swamp, perhaps he could even make it to the 'Nglia seaports.

He crept silently through the wreckage of the Merchants' Quarter. A few buildings burned but otherwise it was quiet except for the odd scavenging looter.

At the Northgate he paused and looked round with caution but the gate appeared to be unguarded.

As he stepped through the fallen timbers a sudden voice out of the darkness startled him.

'Hey bro', y' wanna drink?'

Frankie Lee started and jerked round.

'Huh?'

'I said d'y' wanna drink?'

An outlaw, in the final stages of drunkenness, leaned against one of the broken gateposts offering a jug.

'No man, I ... I gotta go sleep.'

Frankie Lee began to edge away but the outlaw stumbled towards him.

'C'mon buddy, y' can't refuse t' drink wi' a combrade in arms.'

The man put an arm round his shoulder and Frankie Lee gasped as the outlaw's hand gripped his damaged arm.

'Whassamatta?'

'My arm ... I ...'

'Shit, y're wounded!'

'It's okay, I jus' ...'

'Lemme taka look.'

The man squinted alcoholically at Frankie Lee, then a frown crossed his face as he took in the torn and bloody velvet jacket.

'You don' look like one of our boys. You look like a Festival man!'

With his good arm Frankie Lee punched the outlaw hard in the stomach. He folded up and sat down heavily. Desperately Frankie Lee ran towards the highway. He could hear the drunk stumbling and cursing behind him.

Unobserved, he crossed the highway and hurried into the safety of the Northside ruins.

*　　　*　　　*

His arm seemed to be getting more and more painful. By morning he had reached the western edge of the great 'Ndunn swamp. He should have made better progress but he found that his wound and a mounting fever constantly forced him to stop and rest. For a while he had lain on the highway sick and dizzy but as soon as it had passed slightly he had forced himself to his feet and stumbled on.

As the morning sun rose over the marsh, dispersing the blanket of mist that lay on the black surface of the swamp, he trudged on, almost oblivious of destination or purpose, his whole being concentrated on keeping on his feet and going on.

His throat was painfully dry and he wished that he had brought a jug of wine instead of the gun that seemed to drag at his belt. The black poisoned waters of the swamp seemed to be calling him to drink but he rejected the temptation, knowing that it would only bring sickness and death. His mind strayed to his name text, the legend of Frankie Lee the gambler who died of thirst. It was too ironical and anyway, he told himself, the fall of Festival meant that the texts would soon be forgotten.

Deeper into the swamp the highway became broken and rutted; brambles and weeds flourished in the cracks and the rotting hulks of iron wagons littered its length. Frequently he stumbled; the need to stop and rest became more and more pressing.

A twisted length of iron, hidden by weeds and nettles, caught his foot and he fell heavily. Pain and nausea flashed through his body and he lay for a while, attempting to get a hold on himself. He tried to rise but only succeeded in turning over onto his back.

The heat of the sun seemed to soothe his tortured body and the will to rise became smaller and smaller in a world of warmth and pain. Images drifted lazily across his vision. The night with Claudette swirled in curves of rounded brown flesh that looped and writhed faster and faster, dissolving into Claudette writhing on the whipping post, the faces of the onlookers became the animal grins of the rushing outlaws and then they were blasted back in an explosion of pain that spread out into the wide fields of his childhood and then they tilted and he was sliding down and down.

Down into unconsciousness.

XXVI

The young man had been walking for three days. He was footsore and tired and he leaned heavily on his staff. The store of bread and dried fruit in his pack was dwindling and he hoped that he would reach Festival in the next few days.

In the desolation of the swamp it was hard to maintain the excitement that he had felt at leaving the village and setting out to make his fortune at Festival but he pressed on eagerly, picking his way along the derelict highway. He gave thanks that the map his father had given him had led him to the raised highway. The prospect of having to find his way through the ruins and black water that surrounded the highway on either side filled him with loathing.

A flash of colour on the road ahead made the young man pause. There seemed to be a figure lying in a clump of weeds and nettles. The young man approached cautiously.

It was a man. He lay on his back with eyes shut and the young man was unsure whether the man was asleep or dead. As he drew closer he saw that the man's clothes were similar to those of the drifters from the city who occasionally passed through his village, telling tales of strange places and great deeds, although he lacked the usual cape and wide-brimmed hat. The shoulder of his jacket was caked with dried blood from an ugly, infected bullet wound. Hanging at his side was a heavy-calibre pistol.

The young man's eyes widened. A gun like that was far beyond the reach of any villager. Silently he knelt beside the still figure and reached out for the gun. As his fingers touched it the man's eyes suddenly opened. Swiftly he withdrew his hand and got ready to run. Then the man spoke, his voice was dry and rasping:

'Don' rob me till I'm dead.'

'I ...'

'Jus' wait a while an' th' gun's yours.'

'I thought ...'

'You thought th' gun'd make a fine prize. You headin' for Festival?'

'Yes.'

'Don't. There is no Festival.'

'No Festival?'

'It fell to outlaws.'

The young man's mind reeled. What should he do? He had planned to go to Festival all through the winter.

'Where should I go?'

'Go on or go back; it's all th' same.'

'But there must be somewhere?'

'Eternity.'

'What?'

His voice became very faint and the young man had to lean forward to hear.

'Eternity?' said Frankie Lee, with a voice as cold as ice.

The young man looked alarmed and baffled.

'What you mean? I don't understand.'

But the man said nothing and his eyes slowly closed.

Favourite reading from Mayflower Books
A list of established Bestsellers you may have missed

FANNY HILL (unexpurgated)	John Cleland	40p ☐
THE STUD	Jackie Collins	35p ☐
GROUPIE (unexpurgated)		
	Jenny Fabian & Johnny Byrne	40p ☐
I, A WOMAN	Siv Holm	35p ☐
THE SEWING MACHINE MAN	Stanley Morgan	35p ☐
THE GADFLY	E. L. Voynich	40p ☐
AGRIPPA'S DAUGHTER	Howard Fast	40p ☐
THE BANKER	Leslie Waller	60p ☐
PROVIDENCE ISLAND	Calder Willingham	60p ☐
A COLD WIND IN AUGUST	Burton Wohl	35p ☐
STRAW DOGS	Gordon M. Williams	30p ☐
GOAT SONGS	Frank Yerby	50p ☐
GALLOWS ON THE SAND	Morris West	30p ☐
THE FOUNTAINHEAD	Ayn Rand	60p ☐
A SPY IN THE FAMILY	Alec Waugh	35p ☐
THE 'F' CERTIFICATE	David Gurney	35p ☐
THE GOD OF THE LABYRINTH	Colin Wilson	40p ☐
THOSE ABOUT TO DIE	Daniel P. Mannix	30p ☐
HUNTING THE BISMARCK	C. S. Forester	25p ☐
CAMP ON BLOOD ISLAND		
	J. M. White & Val Guest	30p ☐
ALL QUIET ON THE WESTERN FRONT		
	Erich Maria Remarque	35p ☐
NORMA JEAN (Illustrated)	Fred Lawrence Guiles	50p ☐
THE SENSUOUS WOMAN	'J'	40p ☐
SURFACE!	Alexander Fullerton	35p ☐
THE MORNING OF THE MAGICIANS		
	Pauwels & Bergier	50p ☐

Mayflower Occult Books for your enjoyment

MAGIC: AN OCCULT PRIMER	David Conway	75p	☐
ASTROLOGY AND SCIENCE	Michael Gauquelin	40p	☐
THE SYBIL LEEK BOOK OF FORTUNE TELLING	Sybil Leek	35p	☐
THE NATURAL HISTORY OF THE VAMPIRE	Anthony Masters	50p	☐
ETERNAL MAN	Pauwels & Bergier	50p	☐
THE MORNING OF THE MAGICIANS	Pauwels & Bergier	50p	☐
WHAT YOUR HANDS REVEAL	Jo Sheridan	35p	☐
THE GREAT BEAST	John Symonds	60p	☐
A HANDBOOK ON WITCHES	Gillian Tindall	35p	☐
THE MINDBENDERS	Cyril Vosper	40p	☐
THE OCCULT	Colin Wilson	£1.00	☐

All these books are available at your local bookshop or newsagent; or can be ordered direct from the publisher. Just tick the titles you want and fill in the form below.

Name ....

Address ....

....

Write to Mayflower Cash Sales, PO Box 11, Falmouth, Cornwall TR10 9EN. Please enclose remittance to the value of the cover price plus 15p postage and packing for one book plus 5p for each additional copy. Overseas customers please send 20p for first book and 10p for each additional book. *Granada Publishing reserve the right to show new retail prices on covers, which may differ from those previously advertised in the text or elsewhere.*